IF WISHES WERE HORSES

Other books by Keith Robertson:

IF
WISHES
WERE
HORSES

BY KEITH ROBERTSON

PICTURES BY
PAUL E. KENNEDY

A HARPER TROPHY BOOK

HARPER & ROW, PUBLISHERS
NEW YORK, EVANSTON, SAN FRANCISCO, LONDON

Contents

IF WISHES WERE HORSES

Chapter 1

Aunt Hannah

HOUR after hour the train rolled westward across the flat Iowa countryside. As far as the eye could see the ground was covered with a thick blanket of white snow. Several feet had fallen, and under the force of the howling wind, it had drifted in spots until it reached the eaves of barns, covered the roads, and buried the fence posts. All night the blizzard had raged, but with the coming of morning the wind had died and a bright sun shone over the still white plains. In spite of the sun it was cold, bitterly cold. The snow and the cold together seemed to have frozen the world, and all that was alive was the smoke-billowing little train chugging westward across the endless plains.

Stephen McGowan sat by the window looking impatiently out at the bleak scene. He was tired, chilly, and above all anxious to come to the end of his journey. He had been sitting in the uncomfortable coach for more than twelve hours since leaving Chicago. The sandwiches and fruit that he had brought had long since been eaten and there was no prospect of more food until he arrived. He was tired of sitting still and of the odor of stale cigars that filled the creaking coach. Several times during the night he had walked to the end of the car and stood in the vestibule for a few minutes to breathe the fresh air. The car was chilly enough, but in the vestibule the cold cut like a knife. Even the musty odor of the coach was preferable to the cold, and each time he had returned to his seat after only a minute or two.

During the long, dark night the icy winds had rattled the windows and at times even the coach had shaken under its force. Stephen had pulled his coat collar up around his neck and had moved next to the aisle, but chilly drafts had managed to find their way around his head and shoulders and down his back, making sleep almost impossible. With the morning and the death of the wind he felt somewhat more cheerful, but still he was anxious to get off the train. As the morning wore on he saw tiny antlike figures appear in the farmyards, shoveling their way to the barns, battling the huge drifts that blocked the doorways. Later bobsleds, drawn by fat, powerful work horses, appeared on the country roads, and when the train stopped at the tiny Iowa towns, which were about ten miles apart, a few signs of life appeared on the station platforms. Some of the more energetic stationmasters had even shoveled their platforms free of snow.

As the train approached each town, Stephen waited

hopefully for the conductor to announce the name. He had no idea what Black Hawk, Iowa, would look like and, to make matters more confusing, all Iowa towns seemed to look the same. Each had a small yellow station, a cluster of houses and trees, a few unattractive blocks of business buildings, and a tall gaunt windowless building, or sometimes two, located near the tracks and towering above the town like a mountain. These, he learned from one of the passengers, were grain elevators, the huge storage houses where the Iowa farmers sold their great golden flood of corn, wheat, and oats.

The conductor, a tall, sandy-haired man with a friendly face, came strolling through the car.

"How much longer before we get to Black Hawk?" Stephen asked for the tenth time since boarding the train the night before.

Stephen was a thin, wiry boy with bony arms and long, thin fingers. His face was thin and pale, even for midwinter. He had a high-bridged, almost hawklike nose, light brown hair, and a pair of dark sad eyes. His face was reserved, almost expressionless, with the odd withdrawn look of one who long ago had learned to hide his true feelings. His steady gaze seemed to say that he kept his troubles to himself because he knew no one else was interested.

The conductor was a patient, understanding man. He had sons of his own. He had watched Stephen for some hours and knew that he was unhappy and lonely.

"Well, we're about three hours late," he said judiciously,

looking at his big silver watch. "Ordinarily we'd be pulling into Black Hawk about now, and since it's eleven o'clock, we should be there around two, I guess, because the engineer is trying to make up some time."

"Thank you," Stephen said politely, but he drew a long sigh of disappointment. Three hours was a long time.

"Maybe you can find something to read in this paper," said the conductor.

The paper was dated the day before, February 17, 1910. There was some comment about what President Taft had said in Washington, D. C., several stories about events in Chicago, and an article about the unsettled affairs in Portugal. Stephen looked through the paper carefully. Aside from an account by a member of Peary's expedition to the North Pole the year before, there was little to interest him. He soon turned again to looking out of the window. By noontime enough sleighs had gone over the country roads that the pattern of the Iowa farm country could be clearly seen.

"Iowa's laid out right sensible," a stocky man with a huge round stomach remarked to Stephen from across the aisle. The man had boarded the train sometime during the night and taken the seat opposite Stephen. He had promptly gone to sleep and had snored all night, a loud gurgling sound. At first Stephen worried that his fellow passenger was strangling, but after several hours he began to hope that he would strangle. With the coming of morning, however, the man had awakened, and the snorting and gurgling and choking had stopped. Stephen found that he didn't hate his companion after all. In fact, the man was quite friendly. He had a huge gold watch which he kept in the pocket of his dark brown vest. Stretched across the front of the vest and through one of the buttonholes was a massive gold chain from which hung an enormous tooth. Several times Stephen had asked the time, not so much because he really wanted to know, but because he wanted a better look at the tooth. Finally he asked about it.

"Bear's tooth," the man said promptly. "Shot that bear up in Canada about twenty-five years ago."

Shortly after twelve the passenger with the bear's tooth unpacked a generous lunch from a basket. He glanced across at Stephen, and asked, "Didn't you bring anything to eat?"

"Yes, but I've eaten it," Stephen replied. "I should have been in Black Hawk by now."

"Here, have a sandwich," the man said, handing Steve two thick slices of bread between which was an even thicker slice of roast beef.

"You'll probably need it yourself," Stephen protested. "Especially if the train loses any more time."

"Uh-uh," grunted the man through a mouthful of food. "I eat more than I should anyhow."

Stephen thanked him and hungrily began eating the sandwich.

"Like I said," the man observed, spitting out small pieces of bread as he talked, "Iowa's laid out real sensible. Every mile there's a road. Most of them run due north and south, or east and west. That divides the countryside up into mile squares. You can tell by looking about how much land a man has in his farm. It ain't like it is back East, where you have to have a surveyor work for days to find out whether you've got a hundred acres or a hundred and fifty. Every square mile is a section, or six hundred and forty acres."

Stephen had no idea just how much land an acre was, but he nodded appreciatively. "That does sound sensible," he agreed.

"Of course it is," the man said. "And every two miles there's a schoolhouse. That means nobody's kids have to walk farther than two miles to get to school."

"Do you have many storms like that one last night?" Stephen asked.

The man with the bear's tooth finished his sandwich and bit into another.

"That wasn't much of a blizzard," he told Stephen when he was able to talk. "They don't have real blizzards out here any more the way they did when I was a kid. Have you noticed that around every farmhouse there's a clump of trees?"

"I suppose they put the buildings there to be near the trees," Stephen observed.

"No such thing," the man retorted. "Those trees were all planted. When my grandfather and grandmother came out to this country there was nothing but grass as far as you could see, just grass waving underneath the sun like a big wheat field. Those first settlers homesteaded, picked a spot, and built their house. Usually the first year they lived in the barn with the animals. Most of those trees you see were planted as seeds. There were no trees then in all this country except along the streams. There was nothing between Iowa and the North Pole but a barbed-wire fence or two, and the wind would howl down across the prairie all the way from Alaska. After my grandfather made enough money to have both a house and a barn, he used to stretch a rope from the back door to the closest door in the barn. When a blizzard came, he took hold of the rope and followed it out. Those who weren't careful that way sometimes wandered off, got lost, and were frozen to death before anybody could find them."

Stephen shivered and finished his sandwich. The man pulled another from his apparently bottomless basket and passed it across the aisle without comment.

"In time the trees planted by those early farm women grew tall. By the time I was a kid there were big groves around every farmhouse. When you added them all up they began to break the force of the wind. Oh, we still have some pretty miserable blizzards, and if you get caught out in one you can freeze to death, but they ain't like they used to be. Living is a lot softer than it was in the old days."

Stephen was grateful to the man across the aisle, both for the sandwiches and for talking to him. He was interested in what the man had to say, but he thought wistfully of how wonderful it would have been if he were only

traveling with his mother. She had grown up on an Iowa
farm and could have told him all about life there. She
would have remembered a thousand-and-one details that
a boy his age would want to know. He closed his eyes and
thought of his mother's soft voice and patient, understanding smile. He hoped his Uncle Alf would be like her.

He was nervous about going to live with an uncle and
aunt whom he had never seen, but he was looking forward
to being with relatives instead of friends. Although Mrs.
Grover had been kind to him, he was not part of her
family. He had felt lonesome and alone since his mother's
death four months before. Going to Iowa, he felt that
somehow he was going home, or at least to what little home
remained to him. He accepted the numbing fact that there
would never be a real home again, now that both his mother
and father were gone.

With the second huge sandwich in his stomach, Stephen
began to feel slightly more optimistic. His companion told
him the story of how he had shot the bear and extracted the
tooth that he was now wearing on his vest. He liked to talk,
and he seemed to have an endless stock of stories. When he
had finished eating his lunch, he pulled out a plug of tobacco and bit off a generous chew. He managed somehow
to chew his tobacco, talk, and breathe simultaneously.
Words flowed endlessly from his large mouth; he could
even spit without pausing. Stephen sometimes lost the
thread of the stories while he waited expectantly for the
stream of tobacco juice to spurt accurately into the spittoon.

"I was in Black Hawk, Iowa, once," the man volunteered. "I must have been a lad about your age. How old are you, by the way?"

"Fourteen," Stephen replied.

"Well, maybe I was a year older," the man said. "My father was in the stock business, same as I am. He went out to Montana and bought a carload of mustangs and shipped them back to Iowa. I joined him someplace further out in the West and we came East selling the horses as we came. We sold quite a few in Black Hawk. A lot of those horses were as wild as coyotes, but those farmers in Black Hawk didn't seem to mind. I guess they were used to breaking horses."

"Do they still bring in wild horses?" Stephen asked excitedly.

"Occasionally," the man replied. "I shipped in a couple of carloads about two years ago. Some were broke and some of them were as wild as the day they were rounded up on the range. They make good driving horses, those western mustangs do, but aren't heavy enough for some of the farm work. They're breeding more and more of the horses right here. Most of the big work horses have some Percheron, Belgian, or some heavy draft-horse blood in them."

For the next hour Stephen listened absorbedly while his friend told about his various experiences with horses. When the conductor came through and announced Black Hawk, Iowa, as the next stop, Stephen was surprised at how quickly the time had passed. He got his big, battered black suitcase down from the rack and carried it to the end of the car. As he stepped into the vestibule, the sharp, biting cold made him turn up his coat collar and pull his cap down over his ears. Then, suddenly, the train came to a jolting, jarring stop. The conductor helped him down the steps with his bag. He was apparently the only passenger, for the conductor immediately waved to the engineer and with a snort and a puff the train was off again. Stephen waved good-by to his friend with the bear's tooth and looked around. The train went rolling on down the track into the distance and he was left alone on the platform. He was in Black Hawk, Iowa, his future home.

From where he stood, Stephen could see most of the two blocks of the main street, from where it began near the tracks, to the flagpole at the other end. All but two buildings were of wood, most of them with gabled roofs but with tall, false fronts. The bank and a large building with a sign out front saying "Ball's General Store" were built of brick. It was plain that they were the two most prosperous businesses in town.

Surrounding the business section was a cluster of houses, each with a thin spiral of smoke rising into the still, cold air. The town was laid out in squares, a small replica of the Iowa countryside. As Stephen's friend on the train had said, the plan was sensible. Each square block was cut in half by a narrow alley. The houses sat well back from the street and were surrounded in most cases by huge maple trees which now looked stark and naked against the winter sky. Stephen looked at the quiet, seemingly lifeless little town and felt suddenly desolate. The cold began to penetrate through his thick overcoat and the tip of his nose began to sting. He looked about indecisively, and then started toward the station. As he did so, he saw a tall figure hurrying down the street. The man waved a hand and Stephen heard a hearty voice boom, "Be with you in a second, Steve, my boy."

Steve picked up his suitcase and began walking toward his Uncle Alf. With the suitcase in his hand it was difficult to tell whether he limped or was merely carrying a burden much too heavy for him. He had long ago learned to take advantage of every opportunity to conceal his deformed foot.

"I'm your Uncle Alf," the tall man said, hurrying up to Stephen.

He took Steve's hand and shook it heartily. He was a big, almost portly man with a huge handlebar mustache. He had a big nose, bushy eyebrows, a ready smile, and a voice that invited one to be friends. Stephen looked at him hopefully, but aside from an expression around his eyes, there was little resemblance to Stephen's mother.

"Sorry I didn't get here when the train pulled in," Alf Frisbee said. "I've been down here about four times, and then just as I heard it off in the distance, who should come in but Dr. Kirk with his team, and I was tied up for a few minutes."

He took Stephen's bag and turned to the left. He had long legs and Stephen had to walk fast to keep up with him. Now that Stephen was no longer carrying his suitcase, he could not hide the fact that he limped. Alf Frisbee gave one sharp glance at Stephen's right foot and then pretended that he had not noticed. Stephen drew a deep sigh of relief.

"Kind of nippy today," Alf said genially. "Twenty-six below zero according to the thermometer on the back porch this morning. It's warmed up some since then, but I guess it must be fifteen or eighteen below right now. I don't suppose you're used to such cold."

"It gets pretty cold in Chicago," Stephen said. "When the wind blew in off the lake it felt like it, anyhow."

"Well, folks are always saying this is a dry cold," Alf replied. "Dry or wet, cold is cold as far as I'm concerned."

They turned right at the first corner and walked halfway down the block to a small gray house which sat well back from the sidewalk. A narrow path had been shoveled through the deep snow to the front door. They climbed the steps and Alf threw open the front door and boomed, "Hannah, Steve's here. The train finally got in."

A woman came in from the kitchen, wiping her hands on her apron. She was wearing a long gray woolen dress that reached down to the tops of her black buttoned shoes. She was a tiny woman with a thin, sharp-nosed face and jet-black hair that was drawn back tightly from her forehead into a knot at the back of her neck. She moved with birdlike quickness, and her dark eyes took in everything.

She glided swiftly across the floor and held out a thin, wiry hand to Stephen.

"How do you do, Stephen?"

"How do you do, Aunt Hannah?" Stephen said hesitantly, somehow disappointed by his welcome but not certain why.

"He might as well take his things on up to his room, Alf," Hannah said efficiently. "He can put them in that walnut bureau. You show him, will you? I have to keep an eye on the bread in the oven."

"In just a second," Alf said. "He probably wants a chance to warm up a bit first. Have a chair, Steve."

The room held a platform rocker, an ordinary rocker, several straight chairs, a sewing table, a desk, and a long red couch with a hump at one end. In the exact center of the room was a huge hard-coal stove which Stephen examined with interest. He had never seen one before. All four sides were fitted with small isinglass panels about three inches square. Through them you could see a cherry-red glow of coals. The big stove radiated warmth in every direction, and to Stephen's eyes the glowing isinglass windows were beautiful.

"That's a nice stove," he said admiringly. "How do you fill it?"

"From the top," Alf replied. "Burns hard coal. Most days you have to fill it only once. On a real cold day like this, it needs a little more at night."

Stephen walked across to examine the stove more closely.

She held out a thin, wiry hand to Stephen.

"What's the matter with your foot?" Hannah asked sharply.

When his foot was mentioned Stephen summoned a smile which he wore like armor. He turned and said pleasantly, "It's always been that way."

"Humpf," said Hannah. "Isn't that just like Helen? In all the years that she wrote letters to your Uncle Alf and me she never once mentioned that you had a clubfoot."

Stephen's smile slipped slightly but he managed to hold on to a faint remnant of it.

"It isn't a real clubfoot," he explained. "It's just twisted in, sort of."

"Cain't see that it makes much difference," Hannah said abruptly, and turned back into the kitchen.

Stephen looked at her departing back with sudden tears in his eyes. His mother would not have welcomed anyone to her home in that manner. She would have had a warm smile, there would have been affection and understanding. His mother had been ready to love anyone who needed and wanted love. He took a deep breath and somehow found a shred of his smile again. Perhaps his Aunt Hannah was slow in warming toward people and she would like him better as time went on. With the hope, however, was a dark doubt; she would never be more friendly than she was now. She disliked him and she would never change.

"I guess I'd better show you your room and get on back to the stable," Alf said. He picked up Stephen's bag and opened the door, revealing a steep stairway leading to the second floor. They went up, turned at the top of the stairway, and went to a room directly over the living room. Alf placed the suitcase on a chair.

"Kind of cold in here today 'cause it's so cold outside," Alf said half-apologetically. He pointed to the stovepipe which came through the middle of the floor from the stove below, rose to a point near the ceiling, and then made a bend to enter the chimney at the far end of the room. "You get a lot of heat from that stovepipe," he said, "so it doesn't get too cold in here. On real cold nights you'll probably want to undress downstairs 'fore you come up here." He pointed to the huge walnut bed.

"That's a feather bed on there. No matter if it's ten below in here, you'll sleep as warm as toast."

Stephen walked to the center of the room and held his hand tentatively toward the black stovepipe. He could feel the heat radiating from it but it made little impression on the frigid room.

"Don't get up in the middle of the night and bump into that. You'll scorch your hide," Alf warned. He opened the drawers of a small walnut bureau. "You can put your clothes in here. Anything that needs hanging up you can hang up over there on those hooks behind the door."

He walked to one of the windows and motioned for Steve to come over beside him. "See right over there?" he said, pointing slightly to the left. "See that big building over there with the corrugated-steel roof—sort of diagonally across the alley?"

Steve nodded.

"That's my livery stable. Any time you want me, you can find me there. I guess I'd better be getting back."

He walked to the door where he stood for a moment with his hand on the doorknob. Then he turned and said awkwardly, "I'm glad to have you with us, Steve, and I want you to know that you're welcome. I thought a lot of your mother and then, too, I've never had any kids of my own. Don't you let Hannah upset you. She's sort of outspoken at times, but she's a God-fearing woman."

He turned abruptly and went downstairs. Steve heard voices in the kitchen and then, a moment later, the rear door closed. He opened his suitcase and unpacked his few worn clothes. He was wearing his only suit, which he took off and hung on a hanger behind the door. He changed into brown woolen trousers and a red-and-black checked woolen shirt. He hung his overcoat beside his suit and got out a heavy mackinaw to wear instead. Carrying this over his arm, he went back downstairs. He walked into the kitchen, where he stood just inside the door watching Hannah.

The room was filled with a delicious aroma of baking bread and biscuits. It was warm and comfortable after the chilly bedroom. Both the heat and the delicious odors came from the big black kitchen range which seemed to fill most of one end of the kitchen. It was a coal-burning range with eight stove lids, a warming oven that towered up above the stove top, and a hot-water reservoir at the right end.

Hannah straightened up from peeking in the oven at her baking and looked at Stephen's clothes approvingly.

"That's right," she said; "no use wearing your Sunday clothes any longer than you have to. Did you have anything to eat at dinnertime?"

"My lunch was all gone," Stephen replied, "but the man across the aisle from me on the train gave me a couple of sandwiches."

He looked hungrily at the two pumpkin pies sitting on top of the hot-water reservoir.

"Then you won't starve until suppertime," Hannah said in her decisive voice. "I don't believe in eating between meals. 'Tain't good for a body." She opened the two stove lids at the left of the stove and dumped in several small shovelfuls of coal. "I've used a sight of coal today," she said. "Bucket's almost empty."

"Can I get some more for you?" Stephen asked.

"Yes, you can," Hannah said. "Bringing in the coal and cobs each night is going to be a part of your chores. If you're going to be a member of the family, you have to do some of the work. No one loafs in this house. Come over here to the window."

Steve dutifully joined her at the window. She took him by the arm and pointed with her free hand at the long, low gray building at the back of the lot.

"See that gray building? That's the woodshed. Now that first door on the left is hard coal. We use that in the stove in the living room. Every afternoon before suppertime you fill the stove right up to the top. It feeds down by itself. Then you bring in an extra bucket and set it in the corner. The next door to the right is soft coal. Bring in these two scuttles here full and set them by the kitchen stove. Go in the door next to that and you'll find a bin full of corncobs. You bring that tin basket full of cobs and set it here beside the stove. You'll find a barrel in that same room filled with kerosene. There's a kerosene can out on the back porch. See that that's at least half full of kerosene. Understand?"

Stephen nodded. "What do you use the corncobs for?" he asked.

"To start the fire with," Hannah replied. "I s'pose folks elsewhere use kindling, but here in Iowa most everybody uses corncobs. Pour a little kerosene on the corncobs, light it, put some coal on top, and you have a roaring fire in no time."

"I might just as well get the coal in now," Stephen said.

"Might just as well," Hannah agreed. "You'll find a snow shovel out there in the woodshed. Shovel a little wider path while you're at it."

Stephen brought in the coal and cobs as directed, then shoveled a neat path from the back door to the woodshed with a side path leading over to the pump.

"That'll be your job every afternoon from now on," Hannah said when he had finished. She offered no word of thanks or appreciation. "I don't believe in repeating myself, so just see that you take care of all that every night without my having to remind you."

"If there's nothing else, I think I'd like to walk around and see what the town looks like," Stephen said.

"It's bitter cold out, but suit yourself," Hannah said. "Have you got any overshoes?"

"No, I haven't."

"If you're going to do much walking around here, you'll probably need them. Some people are lazy about shoveling their sidewalks," Hannah said scornfully. "Look over there in that closet and you'll find a pair of Alf's. They'll probably be big but they'll do."

She looked at his right foot and then asked, "Can you get an overshoe on over that clubfoot?"

Stephen winced slightly. "If the overshoe is a little loose," he said.

He found a pair of four-buckle overshoes that were about four sizes too large, but they offered his shoes protection from the snow. Wearing these, he went out the front door and walked back the way he and his Uncle Alf had come on their way from the station. When he reached the business district, he turned and walked slowly along the main street.

There were two general stores, one the imposing brick building that he had seen from the station, and another smaller one across the street. There was a bank, a harness shop, a shoemaker's, a barbershop, a drugstore, two cafés, several cream purchasing stations, two pool halls, and two hardware stores. In the next block there were several other stores and a small odd-looking building with a sign "Plumbing and Soldering—Cal Hooker, Windmill Expert." The second block was dominated by a huge white wooden building with a front porch supported by white wooden columns across its entire width. A faded sign of gold letters against a black background hung at one end of the porch. It said "Imperial Hotel. Rooms and Meals."

Stephen crossed the street and walked slowly toward the hotel. The big heavy boots made his limp even more pronounced but he squared his shoulders defiantly. He was going to live in Black Hawk and the sooner everyone in town knew that he was lame, the sooner the embarrassment would be over.

From the sidewalk he was able to look directly into the hotel lobby. It was a large, gloomy room with brown leather chairs and huge brass spittoons scattered around haphazardly but generously. Several men sat in the chairs talking. They were salesmen or drummers who'd been passing through and were trapped by the storm. Stephen turned from his survey of the hotel and looked directly across the street. The building opposite was almost as large as the hotel, but it was a dingy gray and had not been painted for a long, long time. There were only two small windows in the second floor while, at the street level, there were two huge double doors which were closed at the moment. Above them, painted the entire width of the building front in fresh black letters, was the sign, "Alfred Frisbee. Livery and Feed."

The hotel and the livery stable stood about midway

in the second block of Black Hawk's business section. However, Stephen could see what little remained, and there seemed no point in walking to the flagpole at the end of the street. By this time he had decided that his Aunt Hannah was right. It was much too cold a day for a walk. He crossed the street and opened the glass-paneled door to the right of the big double doors and entered the office of the Frisbee livery stable.

He found himself in a dingy room about twenty feet square, in the center of which sat a potbellied iron stove. The stove, although it looked ancient and dirty, was doing its job nobly, for the room was warm, almost hot. The office furnishings were simple. There was an ancient roll-top desk in one corner, a ring of six chairs around the stove, two spittoons, and a bench against one wall. The room smelled of cigars, chewing tobacco, and perspiring men and horses. A pudgy man with thick glasses which made him look like an owl was tilted back in one of the chairs. He chewed his tobacco for a minute, spat at one of the cuspidors, and then said, "I reckon you're Stephen McGowan."

"That's right," said Stephen.

"Glad to meet you. My name's Herb Bainbridge," the man volunteered. "I'm the town loafer."

"I'm glad to meet you," Stephen said, a trifle startled.

"That is, I'm the only one in town who's honest enough to admit that he's a loafer," Herb Bainbridge continued. " 'Bout half the people in town loaf and just pretend they don't. The way I feel about it is, why work when you don't have to?" He grinned, and Stephen smiled back.

"Is my Uncle Alfred here?" he asked.

"He is," Herb told him, "only you'd better call him Alf or nobody in town will know who you mean. He's out in the barn someplace, probably in the last stall on the right-hand side, fussing around Copper Lady."

"Copper Lady?" Stephen asked.

"Copper Lady is a horse," Herb said, "a fine horse, and Alf Frisbee loves fine horses even more than he loves food." He pointed at a door. "Go through there and on back. Been around horses much?"

Stephen shook his head. "No, I've just ridden in a carriage. Once I drove a team a little way."

Herb looked at him in amazement. "You mean you've never ridden a horse?"

"No," Stephen admitted.

"Holy Ned, you've got a lot to learn," Herb said wonderingly, "and your uncle's just the man that can teach you. Now your Aunt Hannah would probably say that horses are your Uncle Alf's weak point, and she'd probably also say that loafing was mine. It's all a matter of viewpoint. Loafing's really my strong point 'cause that's what I do best, and horses are your Uncle Alf's strong point for certain. He knows more about them than any man in these parts. Also with horses, it ain't just knowledge, it's feel. Alf's got a feel for horses."

"A feel?" Stephen asked.

"Just watch him awhile; you'll see what I mean."

Stephen started to open the door leading into the stable, but Herb stopped him.

"I don't know much about horses myself," Herb said, "except maybe which end is the front, but I'll give you your first piece of advice before you go out in the stable. Stay well clear of all those horses' heels. Always stay at least six feet away from the hind end of a horse, and about ten feet from the hind end of a mule or a jackass. When you walk from one side of a horse to another, either go around in front of him or make a nice big circle around his heels. And until you know a little bit about horses, stay out of the stalls." He waved Stephen on through the door. "Go on, now. If you don't know anything about horses, it's high time you started getting educated."

Stephen stepped through the door, closed it behind him, and looked around the big dimly lit barn. For some unknown reason he felt a sudden anticipation and his blood seemed to run faster through his veins. There was a catch in his throat and an odd feeling in the pit of his stomach. The barn was charged with a strange and heady excitement. He had entered into a new and fascinating world—the world of horses.

Chapter II

The Drifter

ALF FRISBEE'S big livery barn had stalls for twenty-eight horses, but there were seldom more than twelve to fifteen regular occupants. Dr. Kirk usually kept two teams of driving horses stabled there, Alf always had at least four teams ready for hire, and often there would be a team or two belonging to someone in town who wanted his animals cared for temporarily for one reason or another. During the summer, Alf Frisbee also kept several riding horses available for customers who preferred riding to driving a buggy. The remaining stalls were used for transients—farmers who happened to be in town on a cold or rainy day and wanted their horses inside, travelers who were passing through town, or anyone else who wanted his horse stabled for a short time. On a Saturday night, when all the stores stayed open and the farmers came to town to do their shopping, the stable overflowed with horses if the weather was bad. But on a summer night, when the weather was good, and a full moon was riding high in the sky, Alf Frisbee's stalls were often

empty. Every available horse and buggy would be mean-
dering along some back country road, the occupants holding hands and gazing at the stars instead of the road.

Stephen wandered slowly down the center of the big
gloomy building. He wanted to stop and pat each horse on
the head and talk to it, but he remembered Herb Bainbridge's advice and wisely followed it. There were gray
horses, black horses, bays, and roans. Stephen paused in
front of each stall, unable to decide which horse he liked
the best. He forgot that there was anything in the world
except the horses and himself. Finally, he came to the last
stall and there was no longer any doubt in his mind about
which horse he liked best, for there stood the most beautiful
horse in the world. She was a small horse with a short-
coupled, well-muscled body. Her head was small and
proud and she had wide-spaced, soft, intelligent eyes. Her
hide was a beautiful glistening copper. Even in the semi-
darkness of the big barn her coat was lustrous and perfect.
She radiated or reflected what light there was like a highly
polished copper kettle. She turned her head toward Stephen
and looked at him calmly and quietly.

"So you're Copper Lady," he said softly. "You're the
most beautiful horse I've ever seen."

Fascinated, he walked forward slowly, until he could
touch her soft muzzle. She stood quietly for a moment and
then nuzzled his hand gently. Stephen started talking to
her softly, only half-conscious of what he said. He told
her how beautiful he thought she was, how much he ad-

mired her shining copper color. He made sounds that were only half-words but she seemed to understand. He was still half-crooning to her several minutes later when he heard a noise behind him. He turned to see his uncle and another man each carrying a forkful of hay.

"Hi, Steve," Alf Frisbee boomed in his hearty voice. "I see you found your way over here. You like horses?"

"I like them, but I don't know anything about them," Steve said quietly.

"You know enough about them to pick the finest horse in the stable," Alf Frisbee said. "Isn't she a beauty?"

"She's a wonderful horse," Steve said admiringly. "Is she a riding horse or a driving horse?"

"A riding horse," Alf Frisbee said promptly, as if shocked at the idea of driving anything so beautiful as Copper Lady. "She's a quarter horse."

Steve took a deep breath and looked around the big stable. "It must be wonderful to own all these horses, and especially this one."

Alf Frisbee cleared his throat and looked at the lanky man beside him.

"Well, they aren't all mine, Steve. There's two teams up there belong to Dr. Kirk. That big Belgian belongs to a man named Hazard south of town, and Copper Lady belongs to Bob Simms here. Bob, this is my nephew, Stephen McGowan. He's come out from Chicago to live with us. Steve, this is Bob Simms who's helping me here in the stable over the winter."

"I'm glad to meet you, Mr. Simms," Stephen said politely, holding out his hand.

Simms said nothing but took Steve's hand in his own hard, strong palm and gave it a vigorous squeeze and shake. He was a thin, stringy man of medium height with sad blue eyes. He was about forty years of age and he wore overalls, a blue denim shirt that badly needed washing, and a grimy felt hat that was pulled low over his left eye. He had not shaved for several days and he kept his face turned sideways to Stephen, looking at him out of his right eye. Stephen sensed that Simms, like himself, was shy and uncertain about meeting new people. In spite of Simms's silence and his unwashed, unshaven appearance, Stephen felt the thin man would make a fine friend.

"Yup, you don't see many horses in Copper Lady's class," Alf Frisbee said, breaking the silence.

"She must be wonderful to ride," Stephen said with enthusiasm, speaking to Simms.

"Uh-hum," Simms said noncommittally. "She's a good horse."

Alf Frisbee picked up a handful of hay from the small mound. He looked at it carefully, and then walked to the small window a short distance away. "That's pretty good hay," he said judiciously. "Alfalfa will dry green, but clover always turns black like that. It's still good. Go ahead and give it to her."

Simms dutifully jabbed his pitchfork into the mound of hay and deftly tossed it into Copper Lady's manger. She nuzzled it for a moment and then daintily picked up a mouthful and began chewing on it.

"I'll tell you something, Steve," Alf said. "If you want to keep a horse in good shape, feed it clover or alfalfa. Now all your life you're going to hear people say that timothy is the thing for horses. That's a lot of hogwash. Good timothy hay is not bad, but the main reason it's become known as a horse hay is because it's not good enough for dairy cows. If you really want to give a horse some nourishment, give it some clover hay, some oats, and some molasses."

Simms looked at Steve with the faintest suggestion of a grin. "Your uncle babies this horse," he said.

"A good horse deserves good treatment," Alf Frisbee announced in his booming voice. He picked up the blanket he'd been carrying and entered Copper Lady's stall. She stood quietly while he adjusted the blanket and fastened it firmly in place. Steve watched with interest. In spite of the bitter cold outside, the stable was surprisingly comfortable. The big mow full of hay above the stalls insulated the ground floor from the cold and the horses themselves gave off a great deal of heat. It was chilly enough for the horses' breath to be steamy, but it was not cold.

"It's healthier for horses if there's a little bite in the air," Alf Frisbee said, "but I'm afraid this stall is a trifle drafty."

Again Simms gave Steve a slight grin, but this time he said nothing.

They walked slowly back toward the office, with Alf

Frisbee pausing in front of each stall to explain the interesting points or peculiarities of the horse inside. Back in the office they sat down in the ring of chairs that surrounded the roaring stove.

"Let's see, your father died about six years ago, didn't he?" Alf Frisbee asked.

Stephen nodded. "When I was eight."

"It's been kind of rough on you," Alf Frisbee said. "No brother, no man around the house, no horses. This here stable is just what you need."

Herb Bainbridge gave a short, explosive laugh. "There's those that might think just the opposite," he said.

Alf Frisbee made no answer but glanced at his watch. "Guess I'd better get over to the bank before it closes," he said. "You stay here, Steve. I'll be back in a few minutes."

He put on his coat, took a canvas bag from the drawer of the desk, and went out the door. Simms sat with his chair tipped back against the wall, his hat pulled down low over his eyes. There was silence for a moment and then Herb Bainbridge asked, "Well, what'd you think of the horses, Steve?"

"I liked them all," Steve said enthusiastically, "especially Copper Lady. Just what is a quarter horse, anyhow?"

He addressed the question to Robert Simms, who raised the brim of his hat from his eyes and turned toward Steve. For the first time Stephen saw the man full face in a reasonable light and the sight was a distinct shock. Simms's face was disfigured by an ugly purple birthmark which stretched from the hairline above the left eye down across the side of his face to his chin. It came almost to his nose in front and reached back as far as his left ear. It made the man appear as though the entire left side of his face was a huge livid wound. Even though he felt resentful when other people appeared surprised or shocked at his crippled foot, Stephen could not prevent a start at the sight of the ugly disfiguring birthmark. If Simms noticed, he gave no sign of it.

"A quarter horse is a horse that's bred to race short distances," he told Steve. "It's one of the best and most useful little horses this country has ever had. They've been used for pack horses, for work horses, for driving, they make a good trail horse, and they're some of the best cow ponies the West has ever known. The way they got the name 'quarter horse' is that they're used for racing the quarter mile. They start fast and have a lot of speed for a short distance."

"Whenever a new section of this country got settled and men started racing horses, the quarter-mile race was always the first race," Herb Bainbridge said. "Back in New England, in the early days of the country, in Virginia, North Carolina, always the quarter-mile race came first. When the settlers had cleared enough land to plant their crops it wasn't too much of a job to clear a straight quarter-mile track. All you had to do was find a piece of road a quarter of a mile long without a turn and everything was set for a race. They could use their riding horses, their trail horses, or plow horses; any of them had endurance enough for a quarter of a mile run. Usually there were only a few horses, most often only two, in a quarter of a mile race. Two men just got together, got to arguing about which horse was fastest. They settled it with a private race. Then, as people got more money and the land got more settled, they built big round oval tracks and cluttered up their racing with a lot of rules and regulations, and the thoroughbred horse came in. The little quarter horse just kept moving on to the frontier. Quarter-horse racing will probably be on its way out around here before too many years, but I guess there'll always be quarter horses, as long as there are cow ponies out in the West."

"I thought you didn't know anything about horses," Simms said in mild surprise.

"I don't know anything about horses," Herb Bainbridge answered, "just about the history of horses."

Alf Frisbee returned a few moments later and resumed his seat near the stove. For the next hour he and Herb Bainbridge competed in telling tall tales about horses, about the weather, and about wild experiences in their youth. Stephen listened in fascinated silence. Simms, too, was silent. Now and then he would raise his hatbrim to wink at Stephen when the truth was plainly being stretched to the breaking point. Shortly after five o'clock Frisbee and Simms, with Stephen following, went out to care for the horses. Herb Bainbridge stood up, stretched, scraped the remaining tobacco from his corncob pipe, allowing it to spill on the floor, and departed to loaf elsewhere.

Shortly before six they finished feeding, watering, and bedding the horses down for the night. A huge wooden bar was placed across the big front doors, and Stephen and his Uncle Alf walked through the stable to the rear entrance.

"How late does Mr. Simms stay?" Stephen asked as they crossed the alley toward the little gray house.

"He stays all night," Frisbee replied. "He sleeps there."

"Where?" asked Stephen in surprise.

"When it's not so cold, up in the haymow. A man couldn't ask for a softer, sweeter-smelling bed than a pile of good fresh hay," Alf observed. "Of course, in the middle of winter this way, it gets a little chilly for him up in the mow. He sets up a cot in the office."

Using the path that Stephen had shoveled earlier in the afternoon, they approached the house from the rear and entered the kitchen door. Hannah had supper ready. Three places were set on the worn, oilcloth-covered table, and Hannah was cooking something on top of the big kitchen range. There were no frills or furbelows to Hannah's table arrangements. There were simply three white plates at each of which there was a knife, a fork, and a spoon. Cups and saucers were in front of two of the plates and a glass of milk by the other. In the center of the table stood a huge salt and pepper shaker, a sugar bowl, and a plate containing a mound of butter.

"Wash up," Hannah ordered. "Supper will be on the table in a minute."

Alf Frisbee walked to the cistern pump in the corner of the room and pumped a basin full of water.

"Go ahead," he told Stephen, handing him a cake of hard yellow homemade soap.

"What's the difference between this water and that from the pump in the back yard?" Stephen asked as he washed.

"When it rains the water runs off the roof into a big cement tank in the ground called a cistern," Alf explained. "That's where this water comes from. We use it for washing. The pump in the back yard is to the well. That's drinking water."

"Well water is harder'n sin around here," Hannah added. "You could use a whole cake of soap and never get a bit of suds if you washed in that."

Stephen dried his hands on the roller towel which hung beside the sink. Then he walked to the table and stood near his place until Alf and Hannah were ready. She placed a bowl of stewed tomatoes, a huge platter of pork chops, and another of fried potatoes on the table. Then she cut some slices of homemade bread, three pieces of pumpkin pie, and dinner was ready. They sat down and Hannah said a lengthy blessing. As she said "Amen," she looked up at her husband across the table, her dark eyes accusing.

"He smells of tobacco smoke," she said abruptly. "I s'pose he spent most of the afternoon sitting in that office listening to those loafers and liars."

"He was helping Simms and me with our horses," Alf said uneasily.

"If I'm to have a hand in raising this boy, if I'm to cook

for him and wash for him, I expect to have something to say about his bringing up," Hannah announced with tones of finality. "And on Judgment Day I'll not have it said that I brought up a boy to be a livery-stable loafer."

"He wasn't loafing," Alf protested. "He was helping Simms and me."

"Simms should be able to do that work alone," Hannah said firmly. "A livery stable's no fit place for a boy to be spending his time. I'd as leave have him spend it in the pool hall. If he needs work to keep him occupied, I'll find it for him around the house here."

"Look, Hannah, he just dropped in and naturally he was interested in the horses so he helped Simms and me feed them. There's nothing wrong in a boy being interested in horses, is there?"

"Not if it's not a sinful interest like that of some people I know," Hannah said ominously.

"That Copper Lady is a beautiful horse," Stephen said, hoping to steer the conversation off onto a different tack.

"That Copper Lady has no business being in the stable," Hannah snapped. "She's a race horse, and I'll thank the Lord the day she and that drifter are on their way. Has he said anything about leaving yet, Alf?"

"Where would he be going this time of the year?" Alf asked. "The arrangement we made was that he could stay and I'd put up his horse until spring if he'd give me a hand."

"There are plenty of other men you could get to help you right here in town," Hannah said. "I don't trust that foreigner."

"He's not a foreigner," Alf protested. "He's from right here in Iowa, up near the Minnesota border."

"Humph," Hannah snorted disdainfully. "That part of Iowa is filled with Germans, Polacks, and Swedes. Anyhow, he's not from around Black Hawk, so he's a foreigner. Besides, it wouldn't hurt you if you took care of the stable by yourself over the winter. You've managed before."

Alf made no reply but savagely attacked the pork chops on his plate. He cut the meat into pieces as though it were a personal enemy, and chewed vengefully.

"I don't trust people that come drifting into town without saying where they're going or why. What do you know about him? Who are his people? Has he got any?"

"I don't know. I never asked him," Alf replied. "I figured that was his business."

Hannah's opinion of that was expressed by a snort. "How do you know where he came from? And how do you know his story about being from northern Iowa isn't all blue sky? Maybe he's running away from something. Maybe he stole that horse."

"He didn't steal that horse," Alf said with a slight show of spirit. "I saw a bill of sale for her."

"How did you happen to see that?" Hannah asked, looking at him with shrewd, suspicious eyes.

"I don't know. He just happened to show it to me one day," Alf replied. "Look, I don't know a thing for certain about who Simms is or where he came from, but I do know that as long as he's been in the stable he's been trustworthy. Besides, what would he steal there? The most valuable horse in the place already belongs to him. I don't know why it is, but you've had it in for Simms ever since he appeared last fall."

"I can judge a man," Hannah said confidently. "He doesn't look right to me. Besides, I don't like to have anyone around with a big repulsive mark like that on his face."

"He can't help that," Alf remarked.

"Maybe he can't, but when a person has a defect like that, I figure it's a sign there's bad blood in them somewhere."

Stephen squirmed uncomfortably and moved his crippled foot. Alf, too, apparently felt that the remark was getting too close to home for comfort, for he abruptly changed the subject.

"Well, I think this was the last big storm of the winter," he said hopefully, spearing another pork chop from the platter. "It's almost the end of February, so I figure winter's done its durndest."

"We always have at least two heavy snows during March," Hannah corrected him pessimistically.

"Yeah, but they don't last long the way the February snows do," Alf said brightly. " 'Fore long business will be picking up. The drummers will be renting a team to drive during the day, and the young bucks a rig to drive at night. It'll be warm enough for a man to take a little ride now and then. Did you ever ride, Steve?"

Steve shook his head. "No, but I'd like to."

"Well, you'll probably get plenty of chances," Alf said. "Now and then we rent saddle horses just for riding, or to drive cattle to market and things like that. If you learn to ride, you can probably pick up some extra change helping farmers drive their stock into town."

"I'll learn how to ride," Stephen said in a sudden burst of enthusiasm that was unusual for him. "I'm going to practice until I'm a good rider, and someday I'm going to have a horse of my own, a horse just like Copper Lady."

Hannah sipped her tea and sniffed. "If wishes were horses, e'en beggars might ride," she said. "You'd best get rid of your highfalutin ideas and come down to earth. You're an orphan boy without a cent in the world."

Chapter III

The Frisbee Farm

B Y EARLY March Stephen was accustomed to his new routine. He was enrolled in school and knew most of the boys of his age by name at least. He was not at all certain that he was happy at Black Hawk but he wasted little time considering the matter. He had no choice. His home would have to be with Hannah and Alf Frisbee until such time as he could take care of himself. His crippled right foot had long ago taught him that life was not always what you wanted it to be but what you found it. You had to accept things as they were until such time as you were old enough and strong enough to change them.

He went home promptly each day after school and took care of his chores. He brought in the coal, corncobs, and kerosene as he had been told. He emptied the ashes. He also did a half-dozen other jobs that Hannah had since found. She hunted for things for him to do to keep him away as long as possible from that "den of evil," the livery stable. In spite of her best efforts, however, he was usually finished by five o'clock, and then to him his day began. He dashed across the alley, entered the back door of the stable, and was in a happy new world.

One Friday afternoon school was dismissed early. Stephen hurried home, intending to do his chores quickly in order to be at the stable while part of the afternoon still remained. No one was home when he arrived at the little gray house. He was upstairs changing into his old clothes when he heard the front door open and Hannah and another woman enter. He had no intention of eavesdropping but he did not deliberately make a noise to announce that he was upstairs. A moment later it was too late. They were talking about him.

"How is it working out, having Helen's boy?" the visitor asked.

"It's a burden," complained Hannah with a sigh that invited sympathy for her hard lot. "All that extra cooking and washing and housework."

"But he's big enough to be of some help," the visitor pointed out.

"Oh, yes, he brings in the coal and does a few jobs like that," Hannah admitted, "but there's a limit to what he can do with that crippled foot." She sighed again. "I'm afraid he's going to be a big burden for a long time."

Stephen's eyes smarted indignantly. Hannah might wash for him and cook for him but he was not a burden. He did everything that he had been asked to do and he could do anything that any boy his age could. Perhaps he was a little slower because of his foot, but there was little that he couldn't do.

"There's usually a reason for these things like a crippled foot. They're a sign, a punishment of the Lord," Hannah said. "Helen was too good for any of the boys around here. She had to run off with that man McGowan, him with his cane and swaggering ways. What did anyone in town know about him? I said at the time that no good would come of it, and look what happened! Her boy was born with a clubfoot."

"Why didn't Helen come back when McGowan was killed?" the visitor asked.

"Ashamed to, I guess," Hannah said in a disapproving tone. "Running off that way and causing such a scandal, and now that she's gone I have to bear her burden."

"Young Stephen seems like a quiet, well-behaved boy."

"He's one of those quiet deep ones," Hannah said ominously. "There's a bad streak in that boy. Mark my words, Myra! I'll do my best to bring him up to be a God-fearing, decent, law-abiding citizen, but there's a limit to what a body can do. If he comes to no good just like his mother, remember that I told you."

Stephen stood in the center of his room, burning with indignation and humiliation. He didn't care what Hannah said about him, but what right had she to talk about his mother? One of his mother's smiles was worth more than a thousand Hannah Frisbees. And if "coming to no good" meant that he would be like his mother, then that was exactly what he wanted. His mother had made people feel happy and wanted, not miserable and unwelcome, as Hannah Frisbee did. He dropped to his knees beside the hot stovepipe and glared furiously down through the holes in the register into the room below. He wanted to shout out that he hated Hannah Frisbee, hated, hated her! She was mean and spiteful, and she lied.

He clenched his hands and got silently to his feet again. He finished dressing, tiptoed down the stairs, quietly opened the door into the kitchen, and went on outside.

The big snow that came before his arrival had largely melted away, but several inches more had fallen the preceding night, and the ground was covered with a fresh, clean blanket. As Stephen started across the alley he saw two boys from school at the far end. They were pulling sleds behind them and when they saw him they waved and called.

He had no desire to see or talk to anyone at the moment, so he ducked into a shed behind the pool hall several doors from the stable. The shed was a sizable building which Alf Frisbee used for storing several of his buggies, cutters, and such miscellaneous items as shafts and extra double trees. Stephen flattened himself against the wall beside the door and waited quietly for the two boys to pass.

"Where do you s'pose he went?" a boy's voice asked.

"Maybe into Pancoe's," the other replied, referring to the harness shop which was next door to the pool hall.

"Forget him," the first boy said. "We'd probably be waiting for him all the way out to Smiley's hill. He can't hobble along very fast with that foot."

Stephen waited tensely until he was certain they were out of earshot. Then he could control himself no longer. He sat down on the tongue of the nearest buggy and buried his face in his hands and shook with sobs.

Several minutes passed, and then he suddenly became aware that someone was standing beside him. He saw the man's shoes first, then his blue-denimed legs. He raised his eyes and in the semi-gloom of the big shed saw that Simms, the drifter, was standing a few feet away. There was nothing he could do, no way he could conceal the fact that he had been crying. He brushed the tears away with his hand and looked defiantly up at the man with the purple birthmark.

"I was in here getting a double tree," Simms said, shifting uneasily from one foot to the other. He cleared his throat, hesitated, and then said, "You don't want to let remarks like that boy made bother you."

"That really wasn't what bothered me," Stephen said in a burst of confidence. "I heard my Aunt Hannah talking to another woman. She called me a cripple and said I was a burden. And she said my mother was no good and that I was going to be just like her."

Simms squatted down on his haunches and began to draw aimless designs in the dirt floor of the shed with the tip of his finger. "I ain't much at talking," he said, "but

"I ain't much at talking," Simms said.

there's a couple of things you figure out by the time you're my age, especially when you have a handicap like we've got. We're sort of in the same boat, me with my big ugly purple blotch and you with that twisted foot, only you're better off in lots of ways than I am. When you're sitting down, your foot doesn't show. You're a smart boy, and you can go on and get some education and be a business-man when you grow up, a banker or someone like that, that sits behind a desk, and your foot won't make much difference. I haven't a chance. People see this big purple mark whether I'm standing up, sitting down, awake, or asleep."

"But you can run and play games and things like that," Steve pointed out.

"Yup, I guess as a boy your foot would be harder to take than my birthmark," Simms agreed. "Anyhow, both of us know how the other man feels. You never get used to the way people look at you. The best you can do is reach the point where you don't show how you feel. It's when people are sorry for me that I get bothered the most, but that's not what I started out to say. There are all sorts of cripples in this world, people who are a lot worse off than we are. The way they're crippled doesn't show at first, but it's just as bad and maybe worse."

"What do you mean?" Stephen asked.

"Your Aunt Hannah is a cripple," Simms said. "I've watched her make Alf Frisbee's life miserable for some months now. She's all crippled up inside. She's mean, and

spiteful, and niggardly, and she covers it all up with the
name of the Lord. She makes everyone around her unhappy, like you and Alf, but she's the unhappiest one of all.
Have you ever seen her laugh, get any enjoyment out of
anything? She's a lot more crippled than you and I ever
thought of being."

"Maybe so, but she could change," Stephen said. "All
she'd have to do is be nice to people."

"Yes, but if she hasn't done it by this time, she never
will. She's going to keep right on being mean, spiteful, and
unhappy until she dies," Simms said. He stood up. "Well,
you and I both have a little tougher row to hoe than most
people. Since we've got something in common, let's stick
together; each of us help the other one as much as we can."

"All right," Stephen said, wondering what he could ever
do to help Simms.

"Shake on it," Simms said, extending his big calloused
hand.

They shook hands and left the shed together, walking
toward the stable.

"The thing to do," Simms said, "is not to waste time
worrying about the things you can't do, but to concentrate
on the things you can. Don't feel sorry for yourself because you can't win a foot race when there's no reason why
you couldn't win a horse race."

"I'd like to learn to ride," Stephen said eagerly. "Do you
think I could ride Copper Lady sometime?"

Simms cleared his throat. "Well, it's all right with me,

but you'd have to ask your Uncle Alf first. After all, he's responsible for you. Lady's a quiet, well-behaved little horse, but when you're learning to ride you'd better start with something like that old gray mare, Dolly. If you happened to fall off of her, she'd do everything but pick you up."

When they reached the stable, they found Alf Frisbee hitching one of Dr. Kirk's two teams to his black buggy while Dr. Kirk stood waiting. The doctor was a round, red-faced man well in his sixties. He had snow-white hair, a big bushy mustache that would have been white had it not been for the tobacco stains, and a gruff, barking voice that was much more bark than bite.

"What are you doing out of school, young man?" he asked Stephen.

"We got out early today," Stephen explained. "There was something wrong with the furnace."

"Want a job driving me around to make calls?" Dr. Kirk asked. "Give you fifty cents. Be back by six o'clock, I think."

"I'd like to have the job but I don't know much about driving," Stephen admitted.

"You don't need to know much," Dr. Kirk said. "This team will practically drive itself, but when I get out to make a call it saves time if I have someone to take the horses someplace and tie them up, and to move them around in case I'm gone long. I go inside and listen to some woman complain about imaginary pains for an hour. Meanwhile, my horses are standing outside getting chilled."

Steve looked inquiringly at his Uncle Alf. "Sure, go along," Alf said encouragingly. "You won't have any trouble. Like the doc says, that team practically drives itself. You'd better go get a heavier coat, though."

Stephen did not like the idea of returning to the house, but since he had to sooner or later, it might as well be now. He hurried across the alley, entered the kitchen quietly, and found his coat. Hannah and her friend were still talking, with Hannah doing most of it. Stephen slipped quickly upstairs, changed his coat, and departed without being noticed.

Dr. Kirk's rig was ready to go when he returned to the stable. The doctor handed Stephen the reins and, feeling nervous and uncertain of himself, Stephen drove off through Black Hawk's main street. The doctor made two calls at the edge of town. They were short, and Stephen remained in the buggy holding the reins. Then they drove out into the country. During the next several hours they covered ten miles, and the doctor made four calls. While he was inside seeing his patients, Stephen drove up and down the country roads, learning to use the reins and practicing backing and turning. The two gray horses were obedient and intelligent and they were more certain at times of what Stephen wanted than he was himself. They were far better instructors than a person would have been, and Stephen felt quite confident when he and the doctor drove away from the fourth farm and started back toward town.

"Take the first road to the right," Dr. Kirk ordered. "I want to stop by and see old Barney McFee. There's nothing really wrong with him, but he hasn't been able to walk for ten years. I like to stop by and see how he's doing when I'm out in this neighborhood."

Barney McFee lived in a small neat farmhouse that was painted bright green. They drove into the farmyard and the doctor got out and started toward the back door.

"Drive the team in the center aisle of the corncrib there," he said. "They'll be out of the wind and warm enough. You can come on into the house, or, if you want, go out in the barn. You'll see some of the finest-looking Guernsey stock in the state of Iowa."

Stephen chose the barn and spent the next half-hour admiring the tan-and-white cows with their gentle eyes and mournful faces. The barn, too, was a model of cleanliness and order and the cows stood in fresh wheat straw up to their knees. McFee's hired man had started to feed them and Stephen watched him, glancing occasionally through the barn window at the back door of the house to see if the doctor was ready.

It was a quarter of six and the afternoon light was beginning to fade when the doctor appeared. Stephen got the buggy and they drove toward town, the horses trotting of their own accord because they knew they were on their way home. Dr. Kirk's red face was even redder than usual and he was in an especially jovial, talkative mood. About two miles from town they passed a neat farmhouse and a huge barn with a gracefully rounded hip roof. There were half a dozen other smaller buildings, all in good repair and neatly painted. A large grove of maple trees flanked the farm buildings to the north and to the west.

"That's the old Frisbee farm," Dr. Kirk said with a wave of his hand. "When your grandfather and grandmother moved there, the sod had never had a plow in it. They built those buildings and your grandmother planted every one of those trees. Someone back in New York State sent her the seeds. I've heard her tell the story many a time."

"Was my mother born there?" Stephen asked.

"She and your Uncle Alf," Dr. Kirk replied. "Your Uncle Alf was born before I came here, but I brought your mother into the world. I was a young doctor then, been in practice about six months."

Stephen tried to picture his mother as a young girl skipping around the farm. He thought of her walking from the big barn toward the house, carrying a pail of milk. Even in those last few months before her death she had always had a smile for him. As a girl she must have been filled with fun and laughter. She had never been a cripple like Hannah. And if only she had lived, he wouldn't be a cripple either. When his mother put her arms around him, somehow his foot had no longer mattered. Nothing in the world had mattered except her love.

"Who owns the farm now?" he asked Dr. Kirk, keeping his face averted.

"A man by the name of Van Derhoff," Kirk replied. "Gus Van Derhoff." He pointed to a farm ahead on the left. "He lives in that big house up there. A fellow that works for him lives in your grandparents' old house. Van Derhoff is a good farmer. He's taken good care of his land and he's made money. Must own about a thousand acres around here. He's the biggest stockholder in the Black Hawk National Bank. Made most of his money raising cattle."

As they passed Van Derhoff's farmyard, Stephen saw some of the cattle from which Van Derhoff had made his fortune. There was a huge feed lot filled with white-faced Herefords contentedly eating hay from long outdoor hay racks. There was a long, low shed open to the south for shelter. The big blocky animals had thick shaggy coats as a result of spending the winter in the open, but they were well fed and in good condition.

"Feeding cattle out is a gamble," Dr. Kirk said. "But it's a gamble that Gus Van Derhoff seems to be able to make pay."

There was a huge sign on the end of one of Van Derhoff's big barns which said "Van Derhoff's Stock Farm," and beneath it was a picture of a Hereford steer and facing it a smart-looking horse with its head held high.

"Does he raise horses, too?" Stephen asked.

"Driving horses," Kirk answered. "But that's mainly a hobby. Gus likes a fast horse and he loves nothing better than a horse race." Kirk chuckled. "He's made that pay off, too. There's not many men that can say they've made money racing horses, but I guess Gus Van Derhoff is one of them."

It was growing too dark to see much, and the doctor suddenly subsided into silence. Stephen drove on for about half a mile and then he heard snoring beside him. He looked at the doctor and saw that his head had sagged forward until his chin rested on his chest. He was sound asleep. The horses jogged along contentedly and the doctor slept on. He managed somehow to stay asleep even when the buggy swayed and jolted when they hit ruts. He grunted in protest at several of the worst bumps but soon went back to snoring. He was still asleep when Stephen drove through the big front doors into the stable.

"Wake up, Doc," Alf Frisbee shouted, slapping the doctor on the thigh. "You're home now."

"You stopped at Barney McFee's on the way home, didn't you?" Alf Frisbee asked later as he helped Stephen unhitch the team.

"How did you know?"

"The doc and Barney have been friends for years," Alf replied. "Whenever the doc's out in that direction and finishes his calls early enough he stops in to chin awhile with Barney. They have a couple of nips, and it always affects Doc the same way. He's sort of happy for about half an hour and then he falls sound asleep. His team has brought him in here many a time with him alone in the buggy snoring like a trouper. Ain't nothing wrong with it except someday there may be an accident. Something might scare that team, because no team's ever foolproof. Then the buggy could be wrecked and the doc killed or hurt before he woke up enough to know what was going on. That's why he likes to have someone like you go along to drive."

They put the team away and then Stephen started toward the rear door. He still had to bring in the coal and cobs from the woodshed. Alf Frisbee stopped him as he was leaving.

"Your Aunt Hannah will probably ask you where you've been," he said with a trace of embarrassment. "Naturally, she's got a right to know, but you needn't mention about stopping at Barney McFee's or the doctor's going to sleep. There's no harm in the doc and McFee having a sociable drink together. The doc's wife is dead and his one daughter lives way out in San Francisco so he leads a pretty lonely life, but strict church-going folks like Hannah sometimes don't understand these things. It's just as well not to get her upset or the first thing you know she'll say you shouldn't drive for the doc."

"I see," said Stephen.

At the supper table Hannah not only wanted to know where Stephen had been but where he and the doctor had gone on each call. Black Hawk was a small, quiet town and news was scarce. Hannah was quite disappointed that Stephen had not gone into each house to learn who the patient was and what was ailing him. Since he had not, she made up for the lack of details by guessing at both the

patient and the malady. Her guesses were decidedly mor-
bid. She decided that Mrs. Denton probably had diph-
theria, John Barker had broken a leg or an arm, and that
Mrs. Wingate had had a return of her old pleurisy.

"You don't know that's what was wrong with these
people," Alf protested. "Maybe Mrs. Wingate's feeling
fine. Probably the reason the doc stopped there is that her
daughter-in-law is going to have a baby."

The doctor's visits provided subjects for conversation
until the pie was served. The talk had begun to lag when
Stephen thought of another item of interest.

"We went by Grandfather and Grandmother Frisbee's
place," he said. "That's a nice farm."

There was a sudden silence and the air became charged
with tension and hostility. Stephen had lived long enough
in the house to be quick to sense when something was
amiss between Hannah and her husband. Alf said nothing,
but picked absently at a piece of piecrust with his fork.
Hannah glared across at her husband, her dark eyes vin-
dictive and furious. Finally, with her eyes still on her husband, she said in a taut voice, "Yes, it was a nice farm."

Alf Frisbee continued to look at his plate in silence, his
face wooden and expressionless. No one seemed interested
in further conversation.

Stephen spent much of the following day at the livery
stable. He had taken over the job of currying and brushing
Copper Lady and by now knew the little horse well
enough to enter her box stall without fear. He brushed her

thoroughly, combed her mane and tail, and moistened her coat with oil. Shortly before noon he went to the office to see if there were any other tasks that he could do. No one was there except Herb Bainbridge, who was loafing in his customary chair.

"Your Uncle Alf is down at the depot seeing about something," Herb told him. "I don't know where Simms is."

Stephen sat down in the chair beside Herb Bainbridge and rested a moment.

"Well, how do you like it in Black Hawk by now?" Herb asked.

"All right," Stephen answered cautiously.

"Just all right?" Herb asked, peering at him shrewdly.

"It's a lot of fun here in the livery stable," Stephen evaded.

"I see," said Herb. "Nobody has to hit me on the head with an ax."

"I was out driving for Dr. Kirk yesterday," Stephen said, "and we passed the old Frisbee place. I mentioned it at suppertime and said I thought it was a nice farm. I guess that was the wrong thing to say. Aunt Hannah seemed to be mad and Uncle Alf just stared at his plate."

Herb Bainbridge slapped his thigh and chortled. He rocked back and forth on the hind legs of his chair several times and then said, "Well, I'll be a horned toad! What I wouldn't have given to have been there! I'll bet Alf caught it after you went to bed! She probably scolded him to sleep." Herb wiped his eyes with his handkerchief. "It's a long story and an old one. Everybody in town knows it and I s'pose sooner or later you'll hear it so I might as well tell it and tell it straight." He loaded his pipe. "The Frisbee farm was one of the finest farms in the country. Three hundred and sixty acres and good buildings. Your Uncle Alf didn't get married until he was about forty, you know, and he'd already inherited the farm. He was running this same stable, so there he was with a going business and a three-hundred-and-sixty-acre farm with everything free and clear. He was mighty well fixed for these parts and I guess he was a pretty good catch. Without meaning to be too harsh on your Aunt Hannah, why he ever picked her with all the other gals around here, I'll never know. Anyhow, she snared him, and I reckon she had her plans all made. Sure as shootin', she figured to get him out of the unholy atmosphere of this livery stable, with all its loafing and cussing. She probably planned to get him back on the farm and make a church deacon out of him. Course, if she'd managed that, it would have been a mistake. Your Uncle Alf likes horses and he's willing to work around them, but he's not a man that's just pining to work up a sweat. I knew him as a boy and he didn't take kindly then to farm work like milking, plowing corn, and hauling out manure. The livery stable's just the right place for him."

"What'd he do, sell the farm?" Stephen asked.

Herb Bainbridge rocked with laughter as he remembered what had happened.

"No, if he'd sold the farm, that wouldn't have been so bad. Your Uncle Alf has always liked horses and he's always loved race horses. He had a little black gelding which was a mighty fast little horse. He thought a lot of that animal. Inky, he called him. Anyhow, about two days before he and Hannah were married, he got in an argument with Gus Van Derhoff. Gus had a horse he was mighty proud of, too. They got to bragging and egging each other on and the upshot of it was that they held a race out south of town. Back in those days your Uncle Alf was a real gambling man and so was Gus Van Derhoff. Their two farms were the same size so they bet one against the other." Herb Bainbridge spread his hands and shrugged. "Alf lost."

Again Herb Bainbridge chuckled over his memories. "Alf must have been kind of scared of Hannah even before they were married 'cause he didn't tell her a thing about it until after the wedding. Even without the farm Alf was a lot better off than most people in this town. He ain't crazy about hard work, as I said, but he's always made a good living. But your Aunt Hannah didn't take his losing the farm very kindly. She's been mad at him ever since. All anyone needs to do is mention that farm for her to see red. For years she's been quoting the Bible at Alf and telling him every day and twice on Sundays what a great sin it is to gamble. Me, I wouldn't have stood for it, but your Uncle Alf's a patient man."

"I guess I put my foot in it," Steve said. "Maybe I've

said some other things, too, and that's why she doesn't seem to like me too much."

Herb Bainbridge snorted. "Hannah doesn't need a reason to dislike a person. If she's taken a dislike to you, son, nothing you can do will change her mind. I hope you're wrong, 'cause I don't imagine Hannah'd be very pleasant to live with if she didn't take to you. But don't you worry about it being your fault."

Alf Frisbee returned a few minutes later. "You did a nice job of rubbing down Copper Lady," he said to Steve. "How do you like that horse?"

"Better every day," Steve said with enthusiasm. "I'd like to ride her. Simms says it's all right with him, but I had better ask you."

"Oh, he did, did he?" Alf said with a slight grin. "You'd probably be smarter to start learning on one of the other horses that's a little less spirited. In another couple of weeks it'll begin to get warm enough for you to ride without freezing your ears off. We'll saddle a couple of horses some afternoon and I'll go out with you the first few times."

"That'd be fine," said Stephen. "There's no reason why I can't be a good rider, is there?" he asked anxiously. "My foot won't bother me, will it?"

"I don't see why it should," Alf Frisbee said heartily. He looked at Stephen thoughtfully. "How much do you weigh, Steve?"

"About one hundred and fifteen pounds," Steve replied.

Alf Frisbee rubbed his chin thoughtfully. "You like

horses, and you like that particular horse," he said, half talking to himself. "That might be an idea."

"What?" asked Stephen.

"We'll do our best to make a rider out of you," Alf said, "a real rider."

Chapter IV

The First Ride

THE SNOWS melted away, the spring rains came, and the earth turned suddenly green. Blades of grass poked through the black Iowa soil, and buds began to appear on the maple trees. Along the occasional streams, the willow thickets took on a green tinge and echoed to the cry of birds moving northward. The entire countryside, which had lain quiet and frozen during the long winter, suddenly erupted into new life.

Alf Frisbee's livery stable reflected the sudden spring activity. He brought two teams in from the country, where he kept his extra horses during the winter, and they, as well as all the other horses which he ordinarily kept, were soon jogging along the straight Iowa roads, drawing surreys and buggies. Salesmen miraculously appeared as though they, too, had sprung from the fertile soil. To call on the farmers or to move about the countryside they needed horses and buggies. Young men's fancies turned to thoughts of love, but unless a young man's girl lived next door he, too, needed a horse and buggy. Alf Frisbee's teams were in demand both day and evening.

Stephen learned that increased business at a livery stable meant greatly increased work. Alf Frisbee was particular both about his horses and about his tack. If a team came back warm, the horses had to be wiped down carefully and walked up and down the alley until dry so that they would not catch cold. Each strap of a sweaty harness had to be wiped off and rubbed with neat's-foot oil or saddle soap. The buggies, too, needed attention, for while everyone took to the road when spring came to Iowa, the roads were in their worst possible state. A few of the more important highways were covered with a layer of gravel, but the others were made of the black virgin soil of which the Iowans were so proud. While this was perfect for raising corn and oats, it was completely unsuited for roads. With the addition of a little water, it became thick, gummy mud.

No matter how firmly the roads had been packed during the fall and winter, when the snow thawed and the spring rains pelted down, they turned into long ribbons of slippery, slimy, black gum, and the narrow wheels of the buggies sank into them further and further. Within a few weeks after the spring thaw, the state of Iowa was crisscrossed with a vast network of muddy ruts. With each succeeding rain, the ruts became deeper. Water flowed in them, forming little rivulets. The neatly painted spokes of the wheels of Alf Frisbee's buggies not only became covered with mud, but water and mud splattered over the entire buggy.

Stephen soon was able to tell by a glance at a returning team and buggy how fast they had been driven. If the driver was conservative, and worried about his own clothes, the horses would be coated with mud only to their hocks, and the wheels and the undersides of the fenders would be splattered. If the driver had been in slightly more of a hurry, the belly of the horse would be mud-caked, and the underside of the buggy would be dripping. If the driver were really reckless or in a desperate hurry, there would be mud over everything, even on the blinders of the bridle and the buggy top. It would take hours to restore a team, the harness, and the buggy to a halfway clean condition.

In spite of the seemingly endless work, Steve found himself more and more fascinated by the livery stable, and less and less able to understand why Hannah felt it to be a den of evil. He liked the bustle of activity, the excitement of strangers arriving from far places, the banter with the regular customers, and the talk of who had been where and why. The news of the world was passed on by the travelers from such distant places as New York and Cincinnati.

Entering the big tin-roofed barn still sent a thrill of excitement tingling down his spine. He always paused just inside the doorway and went through a half ritual while his eyes became accustomed to the gloomy interior. He listened to the restless stirring of the horses in their stalls and the whinny of those few that noticed him and were asking for a tidbit. He liked to play a game of looking away when a horse whinnied and trying to place it by name and stall.

Alf Frisbee kept a big barrel of brown sugar near the feed bins. He bought it from a salesman who came through three times a year calling on the grocery stores throughout the area. Frisbee was the man's chief outlet for brown sugar that had caked and hardened and was not salable to the grocery trade. There was an ice pick in the barrel and it was one of Steve's chores to see that the sugar was broken into small fragments to be handed out as rewards to the horses. It was a job he enjoyed. He not only broke the sugar into pieces so that it was available whenever Simms and Frisbee wanted it, but he passed out chunks of it himself with a lavish hand. Alf Frisbee looked on good-naturedly, but Dr. Kirk was moved to object.

"You stop passing out so much of that brown sugar to my horses," he told Steve. "It's getting so nowadays when I offer them an ordinary white sugar lump like I use in my coffee, they just turn up their noses and snicker at me. Besides, if candy will cause people's teeth to have cavities it should do the same to horses. I'm a busy man. I've got no time to be doctoring a horse for a toothache."

Steve enjoyed the smells of the livery stable, the odor of hay, of horses, the big bins of horse feed mixed with molasses, and the smell of tobacco that drifted out from the office. He also enjoyed the ring of loafers who gathered inside the office on cold or rainy days and outside when it was warm and sunny. Herb Bainbridge was the most constant visitor, but there were five or six others, most of them retired farmers who had little else to do. They told stories, smoked,

and poked fun at each other. Steve could see nothing shift-
less or sinful about them. In spite of Hannah's constant
critical remarks, he liked them all.

Perhaps one reason why he was so fond of the livery
stable was that he liked his home so little. After a month
and a half in the same house with his Aunt Hannah, he
found conversation with her no easier than on the first day.
She loved to talk but she insisted on choosing the subjects.
She was completely uninterested in what he did at school,
whether he had any friends or not, or whether he took part
in any of the sports or pastimes of boys his age. Her
reaction to information about the livery stable was mixed.
Discussion of the horses brought only cold, suspicious
silence. She was not interested in horses as such, but only
in whether or not the stable was busy and was making
money. To mention any of the regular loafers or the tall
tales and jokes that they told was like baiting a bear, but she
would listen with avid interest to any gossip. Steve soon
learned what he could and could not say. If one of the
horses threw a shoe or was lame or had a cold, Hannah was
neither interested nor sympathetic, but if some salesman
who had rented a team mentioned that he had sold a new
windmill to John Miller who lived south of town, she
wanted to know all the details.

Hannah loved to visit and talk, but her activities were
limited by a self-imposed code. To gossip was a reward, a
pleasure that had to be earned first by hard work. She did
most of her housework in the morning. Since men who

wanted horses often wanted them early, Alf Frisbee had usually finished his breakfast and was out of the house by six o'clock. Hannah washed the breakfast dishes and went to work with a cold, relentless fury. She had high standards about the cleanliness of her house and she observed them as though they were law. However, by working without pause all morning, she usually finished all her household chores by noon. She served dinner, their big meal of the day. By one o'clock the dinner dishes were washed and Hannah was ready to go shopping or gossiping.

By some sort of unspoken agreement Hannah and her regular friends knew what days they were expected to call and what days they were to stay home and be called upon. Hannah had no objection to Steve's being present when she and her friends related the town gossip. In fact, she highly approved of it and often invited him to join her and her callers when he returned from school. Gossip was one thing that took precedence over his daily chores. Stephen was expected to sit on a straight-backed chair in one corner, preferably with his hands folded in his lap, and listen while Hannah and her friends discussed the personal lives of people he had never met and had no interest in whatsoever. Once or twice he had been foolish enough to introduce a subject of his own. Hannah and her friend listened in cold silence until he had finished, and then went on with their conversation as though he had never spoken. Apparently, Hannah considered her conversation both interesting and educational for a boy of Steve's age, and she was quite resentful that he plainly preferred the conversation in the livery stable. To make matters worse, she had no compunction about discussing his crippled foot with anyone while he sat squirming silently in the corner. He had needed a new pair of shoes shortly after arriving in Black Hawk and since no regular shoe would fit, the shoemaker had made a special pair. They had been incredibly expensive, according to Hannah's standards, and she never tired of telling her many friends about their cost and asking Stephen to step forward and show them the shoe. Then she would sigh and complain about the many burdens she had to bear.

Hannah found it difficult to force Stephen to attend the gossip sessions against his will. Usually her caller would say, "Oh, let the boy run along if he wants to." On other afternoons she was expected by long custom to make return calls. Hence, she had little idea whether Stephen was at home or across the alley in the livery stable. After five or six weeks she gave up the battle to keep him out of the sinful atmosphere of the livery stable. She apparently decided that he was a lost soul and in time would become another loafer and liar, if not worse.

One afternoon Stephen finished his chores early and appeared at the livery stable to find Alf Frisbee, Simms, Herb Bainbridge, and two other members of the loafers' club standing in an apparently aimless group near the front of the stable. They appeared to be waiting for something: now and then one would glance at his watch.

"What's supposed to happen?" Stephen asked Simms.

"I don't exactly know," Simms replied. "I've been out back fixing a spring on a buggy. It's got something to do with those two jackasses."

He jerked his thumb at what the day before had been two empty stalls. Stephen turned inquisitively. Standing back of the mangers were two shaggy gray creatures with huge long ears.

"They're donkeys!" said Stephen with interest. "What are they doing here?"

"A male donkey is a jackass," Simms replied. "Most people just call them jacks. These two belong to your uncle. That's why they're here."

"He's not going to use those for driving, is he?" Steve asked in amazement.

Simms chuckled. "I hardly think so. Leastways, I never heard of anybody driving a team of jacks. They're about the most stubborn, ornery critters there are on the face of the earth."

"Then what are they doing here?" Steve asked.

"They're for breeding," Simms explained. "The off-spring of a jack and a horse is a mule, and a mule, in case you didn't know it, can do twice as much work on half the feed that a horse can. They don't use nearly as many mules in Iowa as they do in Missouri, but still your uncle can make quite a bit of money renting these jacks to farmers who want to raise mules."

"What are their names?" Steve asked.

"That big fellow is called Prince Charming and this other little guy is named Little Big Horn," Simms replied. "Don't ask me why."

Stephen looked at Prince Charming and grinned. The Prince had a long, sad face, large liquid eyes, and two enormous ears. One stood straight up and the other pointed north-northeast. His shaggy gray coat seemed much too large for him. It bagged at his knees and hung in loose folds over his hips. His scrawny tail switched back and forth with a sort of sad restlessness, and he stared at Steve as though Steve must be responsible for all the misfortunes in the world.

"Why, Prince Charming is a perfect name for him," Steve said. "I don't see what's so strange about that."

"Well, maybe not," Simms admitted. "But suppose you look at this other little fellow and tell me why he's called Little Big Horn."

Steve moved over to look at the smaller jackass. Although this animal also had a long, lean face, it was not mournful but just obstinate and mean-looking. There was a devilish glint in his eyes, and he seemed much more restless and active than Prince Charming. His coat also was gray and shaggy, but he came closer to filling it out than did his companion.

"Maybe he came from out near the Little Big Horn River," Steve said. "There is a river someplace by that name."

"I asked Herb Bainbridge the same thing," Simms said.

"He told me to wait about ten minutes and I'd know why he was called that."

By this time the group standing at the front door of the stable all had their watches in their hands and were watching them carefully.

"Here she comes," Alf Frisbee said, looking down the street expectantly.

"I got about a minute yet," Herb Bainbridge said; "one minute to go and then it's officially spring and time for the town to wake up."

"What does he mean?" Steve asked. "The twenty-first of March was a week ago."

Neither he nor Simms noticed the increasing noise of the afternoon express known as the Omaha Flyer. It roared through Black Hawk without stopping every afternoon shortly after four o'clock. As it approached the crossing of Black Hawk's main street two blocks from Alf Frisbee's livery stable, it invariably gave a loud, long blast on its whistle. The Flyer had an unusually loud and penetrating steam whistle and the engineer had once lived in Black Hawk. Someone said that he fired the boiler and built up extra pressure just for the whistle blast in Black Hawk, but whether he did or not the result was the same. Other trains could pass through town almost unnoticed, but no one failed to hear the Omaha Flyer.

The first few notes of the Flyer's whistle had just reached Steve's ears when suddenly the air was filled with the most unearthly din he had ever heard. Both Prince

Charming and Little Big Horn began to bray simultaneously. Although the hayloft extended over most of the stalls, it did not cover the two where the jackasses were quartered. Both animals stretched out their necks and let go with the weirdest and most deafening sounds imaginable. The noise floated upward and reverberated against the tin roof. The roof rattled and banged and the whole building seemed to shake, and then the noise echoed back, somehow doubled in volume. An overwhelming wave of sound rolled down the length of the stable, out past the group of men by the door, and into the streets of Black Hawk. Passing horses reared, dogs stopped frozen in their tracks, and passers-by on the streets stood frozen while everyone tried to figure out what great catastrophe was about to sweep over the town.

Prince Charming and Little Big Horn were not content with a plain, ordinary bray. Apparently they had been saving their breath for weeks just for this occasion. Prince Charming's voice was deep and sad with a deeper undertone that sounded like a bass drum. It kept on and on, and the low notes made the sheets of galvanized tin roofing rattle more with each passing second. However, distinctive as Prince Charming's voice was, he was no match for Little Big Horn. Neither Simms nor Stephen had any doubts now about the donkey's name. His voice had both the quality and the volume of a huge brass horn. The little donkey raised his nose high in the air and the notes came rolling out clear and true in an ever-increasing volume. The building actually shook when Little Big Horn reached his peak.

The group in the open doorway of the stable were chortling with glee as they looked up and down the street. With their ears ringing, Stephen and Simms walked toward them. As they reached the open air, the donkeys finally ran out of breath and subsided into silence.

"I think they're even doing a little better this year than last," Herb Bainbridge said judicially. "The Prince has got just a little bit more timbre to his voice, and of course Little Big Horn is up to his usual top performance."

"Wonder if the new choirmaster heard them?" another man asked. "He's liable to come down and try and sign them up for choir practice."

"That's saved me a lot of advertising," Alf Frisbee said proudly. "It ain't necessary for me to put a notice in the paper saying that I got jacks here at the barn. If there's anybody within five miles doesn't know it, he must be deaf."

"Do they do that same thing every time that train comes through?" Simms asked.

"Same thing," Alf Frisbee said proudly.

"How about when that train comes through about four-thirty in the morning?" Simms asked worriedly. "In case you've forgotten, I sleep here."

"For some reason that doesn't seem to set them off," Alf Frisbee said. "Just the Omaha Flyer."

"It's a good thing," said Simms, grinning. "I was just about to tell you that you were going to have to get a new helper."

"Say, what about Copper Lady?" Alf Frisbee asked suddenly. "I forgot all about her. All the other horses have heard that duet before, but she might be upset by it."

"I doubt it," Simms said calmly.

The three of them walked to Copper Lady's stall together. The noise of the braying donkeys might have disturbed the town of Black Hawk but it had not bothered Copper Lady. She was munching contentedly on a few bits of clover hay and she turned to look at them as though to ask, "Well, what are the three of you staring at me for?"

"Are you going riding?" Stephen asked Simms, noticing that she was saddled.

"No," his uncle answered. "We thought you might like to ride her. Simms has to drive the buggy out to John Peacock's place a little before five to pick up his mother and bring her back to town. I thought you might want to ride along."

"Nothing would suit me better," Steve said excitedly.

Stephen had been riding a number of times but not on Copper Lady. As his uncle had suggested, he had started on one of the older, quieter horses in the stable. Alf had gone with him several times, either riding Copper Lady or one of the other horses. Simms had gone along twice, but he had shown neither the interest nor the knowledge of Alf Frisbee where riding horses were concerned.

Simms's attitude toward Copper Lady both puzzled and upset Stephen. As the weeks passed he had become close friends with the man with the purple birthmark. As Simms said, the fact that they were both in a way crippled had drawn them together. The lanky drifter had meant what he said the day that he had talked to Steve in the carriage shed. They had shaken hands and they were friends. Simms did not take such promises lightly.

Since Alf Frisbee was not overly fond of hard physical labor, when Steve worked around the stable it was usually in company with Simms, not his uncle. They fed the horses together, cleaned out the stalls together, rubbed down the tack, and cleaned the buggies. Steve spent more hours with Simms than with anyone else. Simms was quiet, but still he was good company. He was interested in anything Stephen had to say and although he seldom mentioned his youth, he had interesting experiences to relate. He had worked at various jobs throughout the Middle and Far West, apparently moving on from city to city and state to state, as the mood struck him. He seldom told a joke or even chuckled out loud, but he had a lively sense of humor.

Simms was kind to all the animals under his care, but he was not particularly fond of them. This didn't bother Stephen as much as Simms's lackadaisical attitude toward Copper Lady. Alf Frisbee fussed continually over the beautiful mare, worrying about her slightest needs. Simms, at most, seemed mildly interested. The fact that he had ridden the little quarter horse only twice since Stephen had been in Black Hawk was proof that something was wrong. Alf Frisbee not only took almost complete charge of Copper Lady but also gave most of the orders as to when the horse was to be ridden and by whom.

Stephen helped Simms harness a team to a buggy and a few minutes later they started out. As they reached the edge of town Simms urged his team into a trot while Stephen had to hold his impatient mount in check to keep from leaving the buggy far behind.

"Are you sure you don't want to ride?" Stephen asked.

"I'd just as soon drive," Simms said, with one of his slow smiles.

"You aren't really interested in riding, are you?" Stephen asked in a puzzled voice.

"Not particularly," Simms admitted. "At least not like you or your uncle. You're both what I'd call real horsemen. Me, I'm a steam-engine man."

"A steam-engine man?" Steve asked. "What's that?"

"I think the thing I like to do best is to run a steam engine," Simms said thoughtfully.

"You mean like on the railroad?"

"Well, I think that'd be fine, too," Simms said. "Course, I never tried that, but I have run a steam engine of the kind they use with a threshing rig or a sawmill."

"Do you mean that you'd rather run a steam engine than ride a horse like Copper Lady?"

Simms laughed at Steve's tone. "I can tell that you think I'm crazy but that's exactly what I mean. If I could do anything I wanted or own any kind of business I picked, I'd own a threshing rig. I'd get hooked up with a good threshing circle and thresh crops all fall. During the winter I'd run a sawmill."

Steve looked at his companion in amazement. "Well, I s'pose a steam engine might be kind of interesting," he admitted finally.

They jogged along in silence for almost a mile, and then Steve asked, "How'd you ever happen to buy Copper Lady if you don't care very much for horses?"

"I didn't buy her," Simms replied. "That horse represents half of a steam engine."

"What do you mean?"

"It's sort of a long story," Simms said with a grin. "I worked for several years with a man named Wegensfeldt. He had a threshing rig and a sawmill and he agreed to sell the works to me. He kept a good part of my wages for two years—over a thousand dollars—as part payment. Then a year ago last fall he didn't have any timber to cut and was too lazy and old to go out and get some, so I drifted on out to Nebraska and worked there that winter and spring. When I came back the next fall to go threshing again, he had lost the rig, the steam engine, thresher, and sawmill."

"Lost it? How?" Steve asked. "How could you lose anything that big?"

Simms gave a dry chuckle. "He was a horse man. He liked to bet on horse races. He'd got head over heels in debt and had sold all his equipment to pay off."

"What about your thousand dollars?"

"It was gone with the rest," Simms replied. "All he had was a horse which he offered me in payment. Since that seemed all I was likely to get, I took her, and that's how I got Copper Lady."

Stephen patted the horse he was riding. "You mean that he lost everything he had betting on Copper Lady?" he asked, disbelief in his voice.

"He did," said Simms flatly, "including my thousand dollars. Alf Frisbee says there was something wrong with one of her legs." Simms shrugged. "Maybe he's right. I wouldn't know."

"Which leg?" Steve asked.

"The right front," Simms replied. "He spent quite a bit of time working on her, doctoring her up. He says she's all right now."

"I hope so," Stephen said with a silent prayer.

While Simms picked up his passenger, Stephen went racing down the road for a mile or so and then returned. There wasn't much opportunity for conversation with a passenger riding beside Simms, so on the way back Stephen made a number of side excursions at a canter to exercise the little copper-colored mare. He found Copper Lady smooth and easy to ride, and she obeyed the slightest touch of the rein or heels. Although his uncle had instructed him to ride her slowly at first, he was soon going at a fast canter. It was plain that Copper Lady wanted to really run, but Stephen remembered her right front leg and refused to let her out. However, when they neared town he left Simms and went on ahead at a smart gallop. When he reached the alley behind the livery stable, he turned down it and entered the big barn from the rear. As he was dismounting, his uncle came over to look at the horse. He ran a hand critically over Copper Lady's faintly damp flanks and felt between her two front legs.

"You been running her?" he asked.

"Not really running her," Stephen replied. "I did let her canter some."

"I don't want you to do that," Alf said gravely, " 'specially not here in town."

"Simms told me that she used to be a little lame, so I didn't let her go very fast," Steve assured him.

Alf Frisbee looked cautiously around the big barn and then led Copper Lady over to her stall. He stood with Steve, leaning against the stall, and spoke in a low voice.

"That leg's all right, or at least I hope it is. That's not the reason why I'm against your running her. First, I want you to learn to ride well, and secondly, I'd rather be along when you really do let her out. We'll go out to Chilly Hollow Road some of these days. There's a nice flat stretch there and nobody around. The main thing is that I don't want you to mention anything about whether you think she's fast or not. To some people here in town, anything you describe as fast is a race horse. I'd rather people didn't get to talking about Copper Lady and racing."

"I see," Steve said, thinking of the Frisbee farm. "I won't say a word, Uncle Alf."

"How does she ride," Alf asked, "when she puts on a little speed?"

"Like a dream," Steve said. "The faster she goes, the smoother she rides."

"I figured as much," Alf said. "I've ridden her a few times, but I'm afraid to let her go at anything faster than a trot. I weigh too much for a little horse like that." He leaned against the manger and looked at Copper Lady. "I once had a little horse that looked a lot like her, only a different color. His name was Inky. Inky was one of the finest horses I've ever seen but I think Copper Lady has him beat. I've never seen her run, but I can feel in my bones that she could have outrun Inky. In fact I've got a feeling that she can outrun most any horse I've ever seen. Someday she's going to do it, and you're going to be riding her, Stevie, my boy."

Chapter V

Preparations

SCHOOL ended the middle of May. Summer vacation for Iowa schoolboys, however, was a vacation from schoolbooks but not from work. There were a hundred jobs on every farm for any boy old enough to carry a bucket or hold the reins of a horse. There was corn to be plowed, cows to be milked, oats to be shocked, hogs to be fed, and barns to be cleaned. Most farm families were large, and the farmer who was lucky enough to have eight or nine sons could grow wealthy because of his cheap farm help. His unfortunate neighbor who either had no children at all, or what was almost as bad, eight or nine daughters, was forced to hire help from the nearest village. Each summer the boys of every town and hamlet in Iowa moved to the country for the summer. Any lad who did not have a summer job was considered either too lazy or spoiled to work, or mentally or physically deficient. In any case, summer idleness was a disgrace not to be taken lightly.

Stephen had assumed that he would spend the summer working in his uncle's livery stable. Although Alf Frisbee had said nothing, he apparently had assumed so, too. Hannah had other ideas. Hannah's plans for the stable differed in several respects from those of her husband. The argument started at the supper table one evening. Most of the unpleasant discussions which Hannah started began at the supper table. A rousing, biting tirade seemed to help her digestion.

"I noticed Stephen riding that copper-colored horse to-day," she remarked as they began their meal, "and I notice that that drifter is still hanging around the livery stable."

"I've hired him for the summer," Alf said, giving his wife a quick, apprehensive glance from under his heavy, shaggy eyebrows.

"You've what?" Hannah asked incredulously.

"I've hired him for the summer," Alf repeated stubbornly.

"What on earth for?" Hannah asked.

"Well, I always hire someone for the summer," Alf replied with a faint show of belligerence. "You know that. The past five or six summers I've had two men. This summer I thought I'd get by with Simms and Steve here."

"Steve?" Hannah said with pretended shock in her voice. "Are you going to subject that boy to the sinful atmosphere of that livery stable all summer long? Why, Alf Frisbee, I would think you would be ashamed to walk through the church doors on Sunday. You're placing this defenseless boy right in the clutches of the devil, that's what you're doing!"

"There's nothing wrong with the atmosphere of that stable at all, except maybe it smells a little," Alf replied with unusual spirit. "Steve likes the work there and, what's more, he's good with horses."

"Do you expect him to do the work of an able-bodied man," Hannah asked scornfully, "with that twisted club-foot of his?"

"He does a lot more work than a good many men I've had," Alf replied. "And, what's more, he does his work well."

"Well, I think he should go out and work on a farm," Hannah said decisively. "It will be good experience. A boy in Iowa should learn something about farm life, and a summer in the country will be good for Stephen. He's spent all of his life in that city of Chicago, Alf Frisbee. I'd think you'd have some thought for his welfare," she said with the righteous indignation of a missionary. "What he needs after all that city life is the wholesome, healthy air of a farm, not to be penned up in a stable all day."

"He's not penned up in a stable all day," Alf protested. "He can drive the buggy around when we pick up ladies, and drive for others who don't want to drive themselves."

"Well, I've already spoken to Mrs. Corson," Hannah said. "They'd be willing to take him out there. Of course, they couldn't pay him much, but that's an honest, church-going family and he'd learn something about farming from

Mr. Corson. He's a good farmer."

"He's a stingy one," Alf mumbled.

"He doesn't squander his money on cigars and liquor and horses, if that's what you mean," Hannah replied. "Stephen, do you know how to milk a cow?"

"No, ma'am, I don't."

"There!" said Hannah triumphantly. "Imagine a boy fourteen, going on fifteen, in Iowa, who can't milk a cow."

Alf took a deep breath. "Look, you say he can't do a decent day's work in the stable because of that foot. There's a lot less walking around to be done in the stable than there is on a farm."

"I've discussed the foot with the Corsons," Hannah said triumphantly. "They're willing to overlook that. Of course, that's one of the reasons why they can't pay him much money."

There was silence for a few minutes. Alf appeared beaten. He looked down at his plate and chewed on his food in frustrated silence. Hannah's eyes were sparkling and she cleaned up her plate with a happy, victorious flourish. Stephen sat glumly with his fork in his hand, too dismayed by the prospect of a summer away from the stable to think of eating.

Alf cleared his throat and said mildly, "Well, I guess we can afford it if that's what you think should be done."

"Afford what?"

"Another thirty-five dollars a month for an extra man at the stable," Alf replied. "That's a total of seventy-five. It's pretty stiff, but I guess I can swing it."

"Seventy-five dollars a month!" Hannah exclaimed in horrified indignation. "Are you paying Simms forty dollars?"

Alf nodded. "Help's high this year. A good farmhand can get thirty to thirty-five with his board and room most any place these days. Simms is getting forty but he's paying for his own meals over at the café. Besides, with him sleeping in the stable I don't have any problem about a night man. With Stephen to help out in the daytime I figured we'd get by with just Simms's salary, forty dollars. Of course, if you want to have him work on the farm, I can always hire another man. If I'm lucky I can get one for thirty-five, but it might be forty."

Hannah looked at her husband and then at Stephen in baleful, resentful silence. Alf had touched her greatest weakness, miserliness. Her love of money took precedence over her religion or even her love of gossip. She was beaten and even before she admitted it, Alf realized that he had won. He expanded visibly. His big face lost its stubborn flush and resumed its usual good-natured expression. He helped himself to a second piece of pie.

"Well, if you've made all the arrangements there's nothing I can do," she said in a weak attempt to save face. Then she glanced at Stephen and said spitefully, "He probably wouldn't be much use on a farm, anyhow. On a farm you need healthy, strong, all-around boys."

Within a week of the beginning of his vacation Stephen

started riding in earnest. He had been up on Copper Lady at least a dozen times since his first ride. Now he began to follow a regular schedule. The salesmen and most of the regular customers who took out teams and buggies for the day wanted their horses early. By nine o'clock in the morning the first flurry of business was over at the Frisbee stables. There were always chores to be done but nothing pressing in the way of customers until noon. From nine until eleven of each day that it didn't rain Stephen went out on Copper Lady. Alf Frisbee usually went along to watch and advise. As time went on, Steve began to realize that his uncle enjoyed the ride as much as he did.

Occasionally Alf rode another horse from the stable but usually he drove one of the teams and a buggy. Each day they went in the same direction and each day they followed a complicated procedure. Copper Lady would be saddled and then Alf would walk out to the curb in front of the stable and look cautiously up and down the street. Stephen never knew what he was looking for, but whatever it was, he apparently didn't see it, for invariably he would beckon to Steve to come ahead. As Stephen rode through the big front doors on the copper-colored horse, Alf always had the same directions and words of caution.

"You start on out east and I'll catch up with you in a few minutes. Don't do more than trot while you're inside town nor more than an easy canter anywhere until I get there."

About ten minutes later Stephen would see his uncle come trotting out of town in his direction. Hannah apparently noticed him on several occasions and asked him about it at the evening meal. Alf invariably had a ready excuse. Either he had gone out to bring in a fresh team from the country or else he had to drive someone somewhere.

They always took the same ride. They trotted along contentedly for several miles and then followed a road to the right that led down along Skunk Creek. It was called Chilly Hollow Road and the name was well deserved. The road ran along the bottom of a small valley or depression which was the only break in the tablelike flatness of the Iowa land within a radius of twenty miles. Since Chilly Hollow was the only low spot in the entire area, all of the chill and dampness of the county seemed to collect there. The cottonwoods and willows that grew along Skunk Creek contributed their part. The creek was east of the road and the trees cast a gloomy shadow during the early morning. Often when it was bright and sunny only a quarter of a mile away, it was gloomy, damp, and raw in Chilly Hollow. However, the little valley had one virtue which endeared it to Alf Frisbee. It was lonely. There were no houses along its entire length, and despite its following the creek, there were several stretches of almost half a mile that were straight as arrows. Furthermore, the dirt road was little used and was usually smooth and in good condition.

"Nobody lives along here and hardly anybody uses the road so we won't be bothered," Alf Frisbee said the first time they rode along Chilly Hollow Road. "Not that we got anything to conceal, but what people don't know won't hurt 'em."

Sometimes he rode behind Stephen and other times he parked the buggy midway in one of the straight stretches and had Stephen ride up and down past him. He seemed to divide his time between observing the horse and correcting Stephen. His instructions and suggestions were so seemingly endless that Stephen, patient though he was, grew tired of them in time. He mentioned the matter to Simms one afternoon.

Simms was quite stern. "Your uncle knows more about horses and about riding than any man I've ever known. Just pay attention to what he tells you and follow his suggestions instead of being annoyed by them. There are all sorts of riders in this world. There are poor riders who look poor, mediocre riders, and then a few riders who look good but aren't half as good as they look, and finally there's the kind of a rider who's just part of a horse. That kind of a rider doesn't need to talk to his horse. He and his mount even think the same. I never was that kind of a rider and I never will be, but your Uncle Alf thinks that you've got it in you to be a really top-notch horseman. I know because he told me so. You just pay attention and live up to the horse that you're riding."

As the weeks passed, Stephen began to understand what Simms meant. He rode every day and he listened carefully to what his uncle said. He improved rapidly and both Alf and Copper Lady noticed the improvement. Alf expressed his approval in words, and the little quarter horse by her actions. She began to prance and turn playful the minute Stephen was in the saddle. She pretended to shy at falling leaves and jumped sideways in make-believe alarm at a rabbit, and she ran as she had never run before.

Alf Frisbee marked off a quarter mile along one of the straight portions of Chilly Hollow Road and each day Stephen ran the distance three or four times. Alf gave him detailed instructions on how to get off to a fast start and Stephen practiced time after time.

One day in mid-June Alf managed to persuade Herb Bainbridge to work for several hours and he, Simms, and Stephen all went out to Chilly Hollow. When they arrived, Alf drove over to one side of the road and motioned for Stephen to bring Copper Lady close to the buggy. He got down and pulled a burlap-covered object from underneath the seat. Very carefully and tenderly he unwrapped it. Stephen watched in fascination. When Alf had removed the last covering he proudly held up a saddle. It was of soft golden-brown leather, but Stephen looked at it in puzzlement. It was so tiny. He was used to a western saddle with a pommel, saddle horn, and a cantle. The saddle that he had been using on Copper Lady was both small and light, but compared to it, the saddle that Alf held up was a postage stamp of leather.

"That's a racing saddle," Alf said. "It's been a good many years since it was used. I bought it for my horse Inky, and it hasn't been used since the last time he wore it, but I've kept it in perfect shape, and the leather's just as good as the day I bought it. Let's try it on Copper Lady."

"Sure," Stephen said, sliding to the ground. "Only that

saddle I've been using suits me fine."

"It's a nice, comfortable saddle," Alf agreed. "A western saddle is a working saddle, Steve. Take that saddle horn, for instance. That's to wrap a rope around when you're roping cows. If you're not roping cows, it's of no use except to poke a hole in your stomach in case your horse steps in a gopher hole. I s'pose some rubes use it to hold on to, but we're talking about riders, not beginners. Now take that pommel and that cantle that sticks up behind the seat of your pants. They're nice and comfortable, and when a cowboy has to spend all day in the saddle, it's handy to be able to slouch around in it. With a decent western saddle a man can go to sleep and still stay on his horse. Again, that's a working rig. When you ride for pleasure, you're much better off to use the kind of saddle the Easterners use, sort of a flat thing with no pommel and practically no cantle. A lot of people out here and probably everybody out in the Far West would deny it, but it takes a lot better rider to stay on an eastern saddle, when a horse is running and jumping, than it ever does with a western saddle. When you get to racing, there's no question. You don't want the weight of a western saddle on a horse, and the smaller the saddle the less it bothers the horse's movements. Now, this little saddle is cut down to just about the minimum, and that's what a man should have if he really wants to race. Do you think you can stay on it?"

"Sure I can," Stephen said much more confidently than he felt.

Alf removed the western saddle from Copper Lady and replaced it with his prized racing saddle. He adjusted the girth carefully, and after Steve was mounted he adjusted the length of the stirrups several times before he was satisfied.

"I always found that I could ride better with my knees bent a little bit more on a racing saddle," he told Steve. "Take her up the road a way and see how that suits you."

Stephen rode up and down the road for half a mile several times. After the novelty of the saddle wore off, he found very little difference. He seemed much closer to the horse and he had to use more pressure with his legs to stay firmly in position, but he had no real difficulty.

"Do you think you could stay on her if she got off to a fast start and really ran?" Alf asked.

"Let's try it," Stephen said.

"You go on up to the finish line," Alf instructed Simms. "Take the stop watch. I'll start Steve when I bring this flag down, and you start the watch. Time her as her nose goes over the line."

Copper Lady seemed to sense that there was something important about the coming trial. She pranced excitedly and had to be brought to the starting line three times before she quieted down and waited for Alf's flag. He tied a handkerchief to a stick and when Stephen finally had Copper Lady in position, he brought the flag down with a swish.

Copper Lady was off with a jump and in a few short

strides was up to full speed. She went pounding down Chilly Hollow Road sprinkling the ground behind her with particles of black dirt torn from the firm but damp surface of the road.

Stephen had never ridden so fast and he was none too comfortable with the new saddle. He did little urging on but simply hung on with his knees and crouched low over Copper Lady's neck. However, Copper Lady needed no urging or any competition. She loved to run just for the thrill of running. In what seemed an incredibly brief time she flashed past Simms and went thundering on down the road. It took at least another quarter of a mile for Stephen to pull her down to a walk and turn her around. When he reached the finish line, he found that Alf had driven up and was talking to Simms. Alf was sitting back in the buggy seat, contentedly smoking a big cigar, his hands folded happily across his oversized stomach. He removed the cigar from his mouth and beamed at his nephew.

"Well done, Steve," he said. "Twenty-four and a half seconds. For a new jockey and a horse with nothing to run against I call that mighty fine."

"I didn't have anything to do with it," Stephen said. "I was just holding on."

"I think you did a good job to stay on with that saddle," Simms said. "I wouldn't think of riding a horse with a rig like that."

Alf Frisbee chuckled. "You'll get used to that saddle in a few days," he said to Stephen, "and then you'll like it. I noticed you weren't pushing her and I didn't expect you to. This is just a preliminary tryout and a mighty fine one, I call it." He looked thoughtfully and appreciatively at Copper Lady. "I've got a theory that this little horse runs fastest when she has a loose rein. I think she'll do her best when she has her head. Well, let's take that saddle off and put the western saddle back on. Then you let Simms take her back in, Steve, and you ride in with me. I've got a few things I want to talk over with you."

A few minutes later Simms had headed back to town on Copper Lady but Alf Frisbee did not follow in the buggy. Instead, he went on up Chilly Hollow Road several miles before turning to the right and back toward Black Hawk.

"I s'pose you've been wondering why I've been coming way out here for riding lessons," he said as they jogged along.

"Well, it's lonely out here," Steve said. "I thought maybe you didn't want Aunt Hannah to see me riding Copper Lady, especially not real fast."

"That's part of it," his uncle admitted, "but only part of it. I didn't want anybody to watch Copper Lady when she was running. I don't want anybody to know how good she is, or, for that matter, how good you are getting to be as a rider. Stephen, that little horse is fast and with you on her back I doubt very much if there's any horse in the state of Iowa can touch her. Now what I'm doing is building up to something. Any idea what it is?"

"A race," Stephen said promptly.

"That's right, but not just any old race," Alf Frisbee said.

He stopped the horse while he filled his pipe and lighted it.

"Time was when I was a young man that I would have been interested in just any old race, but I guess part of the gambling and racing spirit leaves you as you get older. There's one man I still want to beat with a horse, and that's a fellow named Gus Van Derhoff. Now this is going to be kind of a long story, Stephen, but I have to tell it in order to explain what I'm after."

"Herb Bainbridge told me about your losing the home farm to Van Derhoff," Stephen said.

"Oh," said Alf, slightly deflated. "Well, I guess you know what I've got in mind. For twenty years I've been waiting to get even with Gus Van Derhoff, but I've never had a horse that I felt could do it until Copper Lady came along. Now I think I'm ready, and I'm out for blood."

"Did Van Derhoff cheat when he won the farm?" Stephen asked.

"No, he won it fair and square," Alf Frisbee admitted. "I didn't mean that at all when I said I wanted to get even. The only thing that was wrong the day I lost the farm was my judgment. I still think Inky was a faster horse than Gus's Blue Bell, but Inky had been off his feed for several days and I should have known better."

"Does Van Derhoff have a horse now?" Steve asked.

"He has one that he's been bragging about and racing for the past three years. He claims that it can beat anything in the state," Alf Frisbee replied. He chuckled and rubbed his bushy mustache. "If things work out the way I hope they will, this is going to be mighty sweet, mighty sweet. I can just see it now, the crowd all around watching and Gus Van Derhoff being so cocksure and then you and Copper Lady giving him his comeuppance."

"When's this going to happen?" Stephen asked.

"I figure the Fourth of July," Alf replied. "Black Hawk is celebrating the Fourth this year."

"What do you mean, celebrating?" Steve asked. "Doesn't everybody always celebrate the Fourth of July?"

Alf Frisbee looked at his nephew in amazement. "Don't you know what it means when a town celebrates the Fourth? No, I guess you wouldn't. They probably don't do things like that in a big place like Chicago. Well, out here some time before the Fourth a town either announces that it is, or it isn't, celebrating. Usually the towns near each other take turns. And this year it's Black Hawk's turn. When a town celebrates, they put up all sorts of stands— you know, shooting galleries, wheels that you spin to win blankets, baseballs that you toss at a man who sticks his head through a sheet, hamburger and hotdog stands, merry-go-rounds and rides for the kiddies, and all sorts of silly things like three-legged races and potato races." He paused and grinned delightedly. "And usually, if there are two men around who think they have fast horses, there's a horse race. That's the biggest attraction of all as far as the men are concerned."

"What about the women?" Steve asked.

"Oh, the women will watch, too; that is those that are interested in horse racing, and there's a lot more than you'd think," Alf said.

"What about Aunt Hannah? Isn't she liable to watch?" Steve asked.

"I see what you mean," Alf replied. "No, Hannah's working in the Ladies' Aid stand. She's going to be selling pie and cake and sandwiches and lemonade to raise money for the church." He crossed his hands over his stomach again and gazed piously up at the sky. "And may the good Lord smile on their efforts and send them lots of customers and keep them very busy."

"What time of the day do they hold the horse races?" Steve asked.

"The horse races aren't a part of the regular organized entertainment," Alf Frisbee replied, "but they always happen. There's no set time for them because they are held whenever two men get worked up enough and start betting about which horse is the fastest. Now there's a lot more to a horse race than just running and winning. You have to use strategy when you're working up to the race, and maybe I'd better go into that a little bit with you."

Alf Frisbee liked to talk, and horses and horse racing were his favorite subjects. He paid little attention to the time, and as a result they were late getting back to town and late for their noonday meal. Hannah said nothing when they walked into the kitchen, but she set each plate down on the table with an especially angry thump.

"I saw you riding out of town on that drifter's horse about nine-thirty," she said to Stephen during the meal. "In fact, I've seen you riding her a number of mornings lately. If there isn't enough work in the stable for you, you can certainly spend some more time in the garden. The potatoes need spraying and so do the tomatoes, and the whole garden could stand hoeing."

"I'll do it this afternoon," Stephen said promptly.

Hannah fixed her dark eyes accusingly on her husband's face. "Why does he keep that horse?" she demanded. "He never seems to ride her himself."

Alf Frisbee grew slightly red-faced and squirmed uncomfortably under his wife's piercing gaze. He seemed far more embarrassed than the question warranted.

"Well, I guess he just likes her," he replied lamely. "I keep him pretty busy and he doesn't have much time to ride her himself." He seemed to gather confidence as he talked. "That's why Stephen here has been riding her. Simms likes to have her exercised to keep her in shape. Every horse needs exercising, you know."

"And who pays for all Stephen's time while he's exercising your hired-help's horse?" Hannah asked sarcastically.

"He does," Alf replied. "He's paying two dollars a month for Steve to ride her."

Hannah snorted in disdain. "With the length of time Stephen seems to spend with her he could make twice as much mowing lawns and running errands."

"Maybe," Alf replied. "But I figure learning how to ride would be a good thing for Stephen. Every boy ought to know how to ride."

"Why?" demanded Hannah.

Hannah's question left Alf flabbergasted for a minute.

"Why?" he repeated. "Why, so a man can get from place to place."

"Why can't he drive a buggy?" Hannah demanded. "Riding a horse may have been necessary back in the days when there was just trails, but we have roads now in Iowa. We're living in a civilized age."

"Well, there are still a few people who prefer riding horses to a team. A riding horse can go faster," Alf Frisbee replied. He leaned back in his chair and smiled happily. "There's an old saying, 'The outside of the horse is good for the inside of a man,' and I reckon that's still true. I imagine Dr. Kirk has told me twenty times the last twenty years that I ought to do more riding. The exercise would be good for me."

"And I can tell Dr. Kirk something," Hannah said, her eyes snapping. "If you bent your back a little bit more during the past twenty years, you wouldn't need so much exercise to take all that off your front. There's always been plenty to do around here and at the stable, too. You haven't needed to go out on a horse to find exercise."

Alf Frisbee was in a good humor and his wife's ill temper failed to dent it. He got up from the table and walked slowly back to the livery stable with Stephen beside him. "I forgot to mention about the two dollars a month for exercising Copper Lady," he said, putting his hand on Stephen's shoulder. "Simms doesn't say a great deal, but he appreciates your training his horse. He's not much on riding himself, but he's anxious to see Copper Lady win a race come Fourth of July."

"I don't want anything for riding Copper Lady," Stephen said. "I'm going to tell Simms."

"No, don't you tell him," Alf warned. "You might hurt his feelings. I'll talk to him."

Alf Frisbee went on to the office while Stephen stopped to pat Copper Lady. It was odd that Simms had said nothing to him about wanting to pay him for exercising Copper Lady. There were several things about Simms and Copper Lady and Alf Frisbee that puzzled him.

Chapter VI

The Great Race

HANK LARKIN'S big meadow just north of town was chosen as the site of the great Fourth-of-July celebration. For a week preceding the gala day there were preparations. Wooden stands sprouted like mushrooms in the center of the level green field, a merry-go-round arrived from nowhere, and there were strange but exciting contraptions about which Stephen could only guess. One that looked like an enormous wheel mounted between two windmills was a Ferris wheel according to Herb Bainbridge.

"It's just a small one," he explained. "The first Ferris wheel was one about ten times that size and was built for the Columbian Exposition in Chicago in 1893. I remember riding on it. I was scared stiff."

As the Fourth drew closer, excitement in the town of Black Hawk mounted. Merchants took up collections and decided on the prizes for the races, and the lieutenant governor accepted an invitation to deliver the Fourth-of-July oration.

The great day dawned hot and clear, and as the sun climbed above the horizon it grew steadily hotter. By the time the celebration commenced officially, it was already the hottest day of the year.

"It looks like a good day and a good year," said Herb Bainbridge, rubbing his hands together with satisfaction. "Corn is past knee high two weeks ago and today's a scorcher. If things live up to their promise, it ought to be a pretty prosperous year."

"Why?" asked Stephen.

"There's an old saying that corn should be knee high by Fourth of July," Herb Bainbridge explained. "And another one that if the Fourth of July is hot and clear we'll have good corn weather for the rest of the month. Takes heat to raise corn. On a real good corn day you can fry an egg on the sidewalk."

"Fry an egg!" Steve said incredulously.

"Yup," Alf Frisbee agreed. "I've seen it done many a time. In fact, somebody will probably do it out at the fair just to show off, only he'll use a piece of tin. You can fry an egg on a piece of tin on just a medium-hot day."

"Fourth-of-July celebrations ain't much good if you can't feel the sweat run down between your shoulder blades," Herb Bainbridge observed. "That puts a corn farmer in a good mood and makes him want to drink lemonade and eat ice cream. Yup, it looks like a bang-up day."

Business in the livery stable started out with a Fourth-of-

July bang. Every available team was hired by nine-thirty. Shortly after ten o'clock, Alf Frisbee handed Steve three dollars and told him to go out to the celebration. He put his arm around Steve's shoulder and led him off to one side.

"I want you to go on and have a good time. Ride all the rides you want to, take chances on the stands, do whatever you want, but don't eat too much. It's an easy thing for a lad your age to get sick with all that tempting food spread out before him. Just eat moderate like, 'cause I got a feeling we're going to have that race. You can't ride a good race with your stomach full of all sorts of sweet junk."

"I'll just eat a sandwich or two," Steve promised.

"That's the ticket," Alf said heartily. "I probably won't get out there until along about two o'clock 'cause I have to wait for most of these teams to come back in. I gave strict orders none of them was to be driven out there and left tied up in the sun, so if you see any, speak up. We'll probably run into each other some time after two, 'cause that's not such a big place. If we don't, suppose we meet near that big newfangled wheel thing about three-thirty."

The celebration was unlike anything Stephen had ever seen. The stands and the games had been arranged roughly in the form of a great horseshoe. Midway in the open end of the horseshoe was a special stand erected for the great oration which was to take place at two o'clock. The stand was a platform about eight feet off the ground and above

the platform was a gaily covered canvas canopy. When
Stephen arrived, about ten forty-five, the band of the
nearby town of Winthrop were just taking their seats. The
members of the band were especially outfitted in red-and-
white-striped blazers and tight-fitting caps that resembled
baseball caps. The word "Winthrop" was embroidered on
the breast pockets of the blazers, and on the front of each
cap. The men tuned and adjusted their instruments for
some fifteen minutes while a huge crowd gathered and
waited expectantly. Then at last they began to play a resounding march. The first note was the signal that the
celebration had officially begun. The crowd broke into a
cheer, the dozens of stands opened for business, pitchmen
began their spiels, and the day was off to a noisy start.

Stephen was very methodical. He began at one end of
the horseshoe and slowly made the complete circuit, pausing in front of almost every stand. There were stands with
number boards on which you placed a coin, and if your
number came up on the revolving wheel, you might win
anything from an alarm clock, to a kewpie doll, to a
blanket. For ten cents you could throw five baseballs at a
man's head poked through a hole in a big blanket. For five
cents you could test your strength by hitting a contraption
with a sledge hammer and trying to drive a weight so high
in the air that it would ring a bell. There was a gaily
painted wagon from which a man sold an Indian remedy
for rheumatism, and Professor Flint's Horse and Cattle
Renovating Powders. Next to it was an exotic blue-and-

gold-striped tent with a silken cover over the entrance. The sign proclaimed that Madam Duval would tell fortunes and consult her crystal ball for a quarter. There were several men who were willing to bet that the onlookers could not tell under which of three walnut shells they had hidden a pea. Stephen watched, absorbed. It seemed easy enough to follow the pea until someone wanted to bet on his ability. Then the operator always won.

There were food stands in profusion. You could buy hamburger sandwiches, hot dogs, chocolate cake, ice cold watermelon, apple, cherry, lemon, coconut-custard, blueberry, gooseberry, strawberry, and other kinds of pie of which Stephen had never heard. There were popcorn stands and a stand that sold a mysterious pink confection which disappeared like sugar cobwebs in your mouth. One could drink lemonade, coffee, root beer, orangeade, iced tea, and a strange-looking purple drink which was supposed to be grape but wasn't. One stand sold nothing but corn on the cob fresh from the kettle, dripping with butter, and sprinkled with salt and pepper.

Stephen met two friends from school and together they toured the stands, visiting the more interesting ones three and sometimes four times. Stephen ate much more sparingly than his companions, but though he spent very little on food, it was not long before most of his three dollars was gone. Then, suddenly, it was one o'clock. The band stopped playing and the mayor of Black Hawk ascended the stand. With him were three merchants to act as judges

and Chesty McDonal, who always acted as master of ceremonies on such occasions because he had the loudest voice
in town. The mayor made a few remarks which no one
heard and then Chesty bellowed for everyone to clear the
area in the center of the horseshoe, for it was time for the
contests to begin.

There were tugs of war between teams of six men, each
representing various nearby towns. There were potato
races, three-legged races, bag races, and wheelbarrow
races; and six greased pigs were released to become the
property of the first boys who could catch them.

Stephen stood on the side lines and watched the excitement, his friends having deserted him to enter several of the
races.

The various contests ended shortly before two o'clock
and then the mayor introduced the speaker of the afternoon. The lieutenant governor was a big man with a huge
chest covered with a snowy-white shirt. He had a large
flowing mustache, and wore a black string bow tie and a
broad-brimmed straw hat. He obviously enjoyed talking
and by the end of the first three or four sentences was well
embarked on a thundering oration. He pounded on the
rostrum with his huge fist, waved his arms, and bellowed
mightily. Now and then he would pause to mop his perspiring brow and to look up at the skies above him as
though for further inspiration. He evidently received it,
for his pauses seldom lasted longer than were necessary for
him to catch his breath. As he talked, his face grew redder,

his shirt grew wet with perspiration, and both his string tie and flowing mustache drooped further and further.

Stephen was not quite certain what the speaker was talking about, but the crowd gathered around the stand seemed to enjoy it. At first they whistled and shouted in approval. Then, as the minutes wore on, they began to fidget in the heat. The applause slackened and the shouts lost their volume. By the end of fifteen minutes a few of the more fickle listeners began to drift away. The crowd grew ragged on the edges and by the end of half an hour only a hard core of the faithful remained. The stands began to do business in a quiet, discreet sort of way, the rides began to operate, and soon the celebration was again in full swing except for the music of the merry-go-round and other competing noises. The lieutenant governor did not seem to mind, however, for he continued on and on. Apparently it was a contest between him and his listeners. At last, after speaking for one solid hour, he brought his Fourth-of-July oration to a thundering close. Those who still remained clustered around the stand applauded appreciatively and crowded forward to shake his hand. From the comments, Stephen judged that the speech had been a resounding success. One farmer observed that he had not heard a better Fourth-of-July speech since 1892, while another allowed that the speaker was not one bit inferior to William Jennings Bryan.

Stephen had saved the Ferris wheel until last, partly because he was a trifle afraid of it. However, a few minutes

before three he paid his dime and was locked into one of
the seats. The steel wheel shook, squeaked, and jerked as
he rose into the air, and then, suddenly, he was on top of
the world. The wheel stopped as someone else took his
turn for a ride. Stephen's fear at being stranded so high in
the air in that rickety, rocky chair was lost in his excitement at being able to survey the area like a soaring bird.
There was Black Hawk spread before him, the bank, the
hotel, and Alf Frisbee's livery stable with its metal roof
gleaming in the sun. There was the schoolhouse and the
house where he and Hannah and Alf Frisbee lived. Everything seemed small and far beneath him except the two
giant grain elevators. Stephen gave each of them a nod as
though speaking to an equal.

Below him on the fairgrounds the people were un-
believably small and they seemed to drift aimlessly about
the meadow like leaves drifting in a lazy stream. He could
see the stand where Hannah was working. She was serving
pie to a man with red suspenders and a big straw hat.
Hannah was wearing a bright blue dress and had piled her
long hair high on her head instead of doing it up in a bun
at the nape of her neck as she usually did. Stephen had to
admit that she looked better than he had ever seen her. She
had even smiled twice when Alf Frisbee had complimented
her on her appearance. However, Steve did not believe in
tempting fate and had stayed well away from the Ladies'
Aid stand. He could see enough of Hannah from his perch
in the Ferris wheel.

Suddenly the wheel started again and Stephen felt a

queasy feeling in the pit of his stomach as he seemed to go over the edge of a cliff and then drop downward with startling abruptness. However, he was soon going up again and was able once more to survey the world of Black Hawk, Iowa. As far as he could see in every direction there were fields of green and gently waving corn. Row after row after row ran evenly and endlessly onward to the edge of the great bowl of the sky. It was a big sky, and Stephen had yet to grow used to it. He did not know whether it was the flatness, or the air, or the fact that there were no buildings or hills to obstruct his view, but the sky was much bigger than it had been in Chicago. The sky was big enough from the back of a horse, but from his seat high on the top of the Ferris wheel it was enormous.

The ride finally ended, and Stephen stepped down from his seat into the everyday world. He glanced at a clock at a nearby stand and saw that it was four minutes after three. He looked around carefully, but he saw nothing of his uncle until a hand was placed on his shoulder. He turned and for a moment failed to recognize the owner of the hand.

He had never seen Alf Frisbee so dressed up, even to go to church. Alf was wearing a white silk shirt, a red bow tie, and a light-brown suit that Stephen had never seen before. He was smoking a huge cigar and appeared to be in the best of spirits. He led Stephen off to one side and then looked around cautiously.

"Gus Van Derhoff has his horse here and he's looking for a race," he said happily. "I'm going to mosey over to where he is and then kind of ease into the subject. You just kind of hang around, not too close but where I can spot you when I want to. Now are you all clear on the strategy?"

"I think so," Stephen replied. "You'll have a chance to give me my last-minute instructions, won't you, before we start?"

"That's right," Alf said. "But I hope everything will go just as we planned."

Alf Frisbee found Gus Van Derhoff at a root-beer stand near the band platform. The Black Hawk band, which was to play for the next two hours, had not yet appeared and there was reasonable quiet.

Gus Van Derhoff was a huge barrel-chested man with a large jolly face. He laughed easily, and good-natured wrinkles extended from the corners of his eyes and his mouth into his fleshy face. He had a huge voice, a huge appetite, and a huge gusto for life. When he saw Alf Frisbee he roared out an invitation to join him in a mug of root beer. Alf accepted.

"Well, it's a nice celebration," Alf observed. "Not too much excitement."

"Not like the old days when we were young, eh, Alf?" Gus roared. "We'd have put some spirit into the celebration, tossed a few firecrackers at the speaker, raised a little hell."

Alf Frisbee grinned. "I never will forget old Senator Gerald when that firecracker went off right at his feet. Did you or Curly McNeil throw it?"

Gus roared with laughter. "You know perfectly well who threw it. I held the match and you threw the fire-cracker." He took a sip of his root beer and looked around at the crowd. "Of course, the excitement I miss is not things like that but a good race. I guess the racing spirit's gone out of Black Hawk."

"There aren't any good horses to race," Alf observed with a shrug.

"You mean there's only one good horse," Gus corrected. "But it takes more than one horse to make a race."

"What's the one good horse?" Alf asked derisively.

"Mine," bellowed Gus. "Red Duke. The trouble is he's so much better than the other nags around here that I can't get anybody to race me."

"He must have improved a lot in the last couple of years," Alf observed mildly.

"What do you mean?" Gus demanded.

"Red Duke's a good horse," Alf admitted judiciously, "but just a fair horse, nothing unusual."

Gus Van Derhoff banged his root-beer mug down on the counter and appealed to three or four men standing near by. "Did you hear that? Alf Frisbee, the great judge of horseflesh, says that Red Duke is a fair horse." Gus roared with laughter. "Then every other horse around these parts must be poor to awful, 'cause they're certainly no competition."

"Oh, I don't know," Alf said. "There's probably plenty that can beat him."

"Well, produce one, just one," Gus said.

"If you've got Red Duke here, I'd like to take a look at him," Alf suggested.

"Sure thing."

With about fifteen men following them, they walked to the road and crossed it to the nearby grove of trees where all the horses were tethered. Van Derhoff's horse Red Duke was standing in the shade of a huge oak tree.

Red Duke was a beautiful horse, there was little doubt about that. Stephen looked at him admiringly. He was somewhat larger than Copper Lady, with a broad chest, trim, smooth legs, and an intelligent, small head. His red coat was sleek and shiny. Stephen walked around him several times and tried to be impartial in his judgment. Red Duke was a fine horse but there was something lacking, something that Copper Lady possessed that this horse did not. It was not that Copper Lady was more delicately built or anything that Stephen could put his finger on. Nevertheless, he knew it was there. Red Duke did not have the fire, the spirit, or the quality of Copper Lady.

"Let's see him in action," Alf Frisbee suggested.

"Saddle him up, Jimmy, will you?" Van Derhoff asked.

Jimmy was a small, wiry man whom Stephen judged to be about forty-five years of age. He was not much taller than Stephen and probably not a great deal heavier.

Alf Frisbee seemed to stroll about aimlessly, but he paused for a moment beside Stephen.

"Jimmy's the man I've been telling you about," he said out of the corner of his mouth. "He's been with Van Derhoff for years. He knows how to ride and he's tricky."

A small, light saddle was soon placed on Red Duke's back and Jimmy mounted. He took Red Duke through the gate, trotted up the road a short distance, and then came back at a moderate canter.

"He's a nice-looking horse, I've got to admit that," Alf Frisbee said. "Of course, he isn't in very good condition."

"What's wrong with his condition?" Gus demanded.

"Well," Alf Frisbee hedged, "nothing that I can put my finger on, exactly. It's just that he looks a little sluggish. Of course, he's probably naturally a little sluggish."

"Sluggish!" roared Gus. "If that horse is sluggish I'd like to see a fast one."

"He doesn't compare with Inky, that little black I used to have," Alf observed.

Gus Van Derhoff gave a hoot of derision. "As I recall, you lost a race or two with Inky. Anyhow, what I want you to do is to produce a live horse that'll give Red Duke some competition—a horse that'll even make him stretch his legs a little."

"Well, I just can't think of one at the minute," Alf Frisbee said lamely, "but there's plenty around. I guess I'll be getting back to the celebration."

He started ambling toward the road while Gus Van Derhoff howled with laughter. Alf had gone perhaps thirty feet when he turned and looked at Gus.

"Give me two lengths and I'll dig up a horse someplace."

"What horse?" Gus asked, sudden caution entering his voice.

Alf Frisbee hesitated. "Well, the fellow that works for me down at the stables has a fair-looking horse, and, like I said, Red Duke doesn't look like he's in such good condition."

"How much?" Gus Van Derhoff asked.

"Well, I'm not much of a betting man any more," Alf replied. "Twenty dollars?"

Gus Van Derhoff slapped his thigh and howled again with laughter. "Twenty dollars! Why, it isn't worth getting a horse all lathered up for twenty dollars."

"All right then," Alf said in annoyance, "make it fifty."

"That's still mighty small," Gus Van Derhoff said, "but you're on."

"And I get two lengths?" Alf asked.

"All right, you get two lengths," Gus said with a wave of his hand.

Alf Frisbee turned and looked around, his eyes lighting on Stephen as though seeing him for the first time.

"Steve, would you go down to the stable and ask Simms if he'd like to race his horse? You know where the racing saddle is. Tell him to put that on and bring it out here if he's interested. Tell him I've got a little money bet on him and I'm sure he'll come."

"All right," said Stephen. "Can I come back and see the race?"

"Sure," Alf said. "I think you'll find old Ike helping

Simms. He can take care of the stable."

In fifteen minutes Stephen was back astride Copper Lady. He rode up to where Alf Frisbee and Gus Van Derhoff and a group of men were waiting near the grove.

"I couldn't find Simms," he said, "so I brought her out myself. Ike didn't know where Simms was."

Stephen had gone over the lines two or three times with his uncle, but even so it was difficult to hide a smile as they went through their act.

"That kind of throws a hitch in things," Alf Frisbee said. "I'm a little heavy to ride her myself. Wonder if Simms is over at the celebration someplace?"

"Let me ride her," Stephen urged.

Alf Frisbee chuckled indulgently. "I guess you'd like to ride her, wouldn't you? However, this is a race, and I've got a little money bet with Gus here."

"I can ride her," Stephen urged. "She'll go fast for me."

It was difficult to tell just how much Gus Van Derhoff was taken in by their little act. He was examining Copper Lady critically, and it was obvious from his expression that he realized that she was no ordinary horse. He looked at Alf Frisbee suspiciously.

"Are you pulling something? Asking two lengths?"

"You know I wouldn't take advantage of you," Alf protested.

"Not much, you wouldn't," Gus snorted. "I've raced with you before."

"Do you want to back out?" Alf Frisbee asked.

"No, I made an agreement, and I'll stick by my word," Gus replied.

"I don't like to start a race unless everybody feels everything's fair and square," Alf Frisbee said piously. "I'll tell you what I'll do. You give me two lengths and I'll let the kid here ride her. After all, an experienced rider has at least two lengths' advantage over a youngster like Steve."

"It's a deal," said Gus Van Derhoff heartily, holding out his hand. With Stephen astride Copper Lady and Jimmy on Red Duke the two horses were led to the dirt road separating the Larkin meadow from the grove of trees. In some mysterious manner the word had spread that there was to be a horse race, and by the time the course had been measured and the starting line had been set, a crowd of at least a hundred men lined the road. Stephen's horse was led two lengths ahead of Red Duke and a volunteer was accepted as a starter. Gus Van Derhoff produced a starting flag and all the necessary preparations were made. In a surprisingly short time, Stephen was crouched tensely over Copper Lady's back waiting for the flag to drop.

There was almost complete silence for fifteen seconds before the race began and then the air was filled with shouts as the flag went down. Stephen had gone over what he was to do with Alf and he had rehearsed it with Copper Lady several times, and even in the excitement of the actual race he was calm and certain. He deliberately held Copper Lady in tightly, causing her to get off to a slow start. To the watching men it looked exactly as Alf Frisbee intended.

Either Stephen was an inexperienced rider, or Copper Lady was a slow starter. Whatever the reason, Red Duke gained one of the two lengths before the race had really begun.

Stephen crouched low over Copper Lady's withers, bending his neck so that he could see the ground by his horse's pounding hind hoofs. Alf Frisbee was right. It was not at all difficult to follow his instructions. Stephen kept a firm grip on Copper Lady and waited while the sound of Red Duke's hoofs grew closer and closer. By the midway mark of the race Red Duke's head was even with Copper Lady's haunches and he was gaining. Slightly, almost imperceptibly, Stephen eased Copper Lady's reins and pressed her sides with his knees. She responded by slightly increasing her speed. Red Duke increased his also, and they held their same positions. Twice more Stephen eased his grip and once he spoke to his horse. Then, suddenly, the race was over and he was still ahead by at least half a length. He scarcely heard the cheer that went up from the watching crowd. Stephen rode back to the starting line and listened for several minutes while Alf Frisbee gloated over Gus Van Derhoff. Then, suddenly, Simms appeared in the crowd. His part, too, had been carefully rehearsed.

"I took the liberty of racing your horse, Simms," Alf Frisbee told him. "I hope you don't mind."

"Not at all," said Simms. "I hear the boy won."

"Yup, rode like a veteran," Alf boasted. "That was a good race, Steve."

She responded by slightly increasing her speed.

"Shall I take Copper Lady back to the stable?" Stephen asked.

"Might as well," Alf Frisbee said in a loud voice. "There's not any competition around here."

"Don't be in a hurry," Gus Van Derhoff said. "Maybe you'd like to see if you can repeat that."

"Think you can, Steve?" Alf asked.

"Sure," Steve replied.

"All right, same race, same conditions, same bet," Alf announced.

"Without the two-length handicap," Gus Van Derhoff said firmly.

"I thought you said repeat it?" Alf protested. "Copper Lady here won by only half a length, so without the two lengths' start she'd have lost by a length and a half."

"Then you admit that Red Duke's the better horse?" Gus asked.

"I don't admit anything of the kind," Alf Frisbee replied hotly.

"Then if she's at all a match for Red Duke, you ought to be willing to race her on even terms."

"But you've got an experienced rider in Jimmy there. Steve's just a kid."

"All right, put your man Simms up," Van Derhoff replied.

"How about it, Simms?" Alf asked.

"Sorry, but I've got a sore back," Simms replied, putting his hand on his back and grimacing. "I got a kink in it from lifting that buggy around yesterday."

"I can beat him without the two lengths," Stephen said enthusiastically.

"I think you're a little bit overconfident," Alf said judiciously.

"All right, if you're afraid, go ahead and back out," Van Derhoff said with a wave of his hand.

"I'm not backing down," Alf said hotly. "I guess I haven't anything to lose except your money anyhow, so if you want to do it again without the two lengths, it's all right with me."

They shook hands, and then Van Derhoff went off to one side to talk to Jimmy while Alf Frisbee and Simms walked away a few feet with Stephen.

"Did you have to let her out much?" Alf Frisbee asked.

Stephen shook his head. "No, she had a lot of speed left. She can beat Red Duke any time."

"Don't be too confident," Alf warned. "Gus Van Derhoff is foxy, too. He may have told Jimmy not to beat you. This race will tell the story. Let him get off to a faster start than you do, then gain on him and beat him by just a nose."

By the time the second race began, the crowd had doubled in size and stood three or four deep on both sides of the road near the finish line. As Stephen rode to the start he saw others hurrying to see the race.

This time he did not hold Copper Lady so tightly but he delayed her start slightly, giving Red Duke about three quarters of a length advantage. As the two horses thundered down the short course, Stephen watched the horse and rider ahead of him closely. He was in a much better position to judge their performance this time. Jimmy had a short quirt and he was using it. It was possible that Jimmy had allowed Red Duke to be beaten in the race before, but this time he was out to win.

Stephen held the same position, three quarters of a length behind, until they had gone roughly half the distance. Then he loosened Copper Lady's reins slightly and touched her with his heels. She responded quickly and began to gain. In fact, she gained too rapidly and he had to increase the pressure on the reins slightly. Slowly but surely she overhauled the horse ahead. It was impossible to do exactly as Alf Frisbee had instructed but Stephen came close. When they thundered across the finish line, he was less than half a length ahead of Red Duke. He let Copper Lady slow to a canter and then turned her and headed back toward the finish line while he listened to the cheers of the crowd.

Alf Frisbee was gloating in earnest this time.

"I thought you said you had a race horse," he said to Gus Van Derhoff. "Why, this little mare can beat that nag of yours any time and any place."

"It was close," Gus Van Derhoff said grumpily.

"In case you haven't heard, the horse ahead wins the race even if it's by a bump on the end of his nose," Alf said derisively. He turned to the crowd and said loudly, "Gus here said earlier this afternoon that there was only one horse around these parts. He was right, only it isn't his horse."

The crowd roared with laughter while Gus Van Derhoff glowered. He motioned to Jimmy, who dismounted from Red Duke, and the two men walked over and conferred together earnestly.

"He's trying to work out an alibi with Jimmy," Alf Frisbee said. "Come on, Gus," he called, "just admit it. Your horse is outclassed."

Gus Van Derhoff continued to talk to his rider. Stephen dismounted and with Simms walked over to the shade of the nearest tree.

"Alf doesn't want to talk to you himself," Simms whispered. "He wants to appear so cocksure that he doesn't even have to talk to his rider. He asked me to find out what you think."

"Copper Lady can beat him," Stephen said. "There isn't a doubt about it."

"You're sure now?" Simms asked anxiously. "Alf's going to plunge on this."

"I'm as certain as I can ever be of anything," Stephen replied. "Uncle Alf was right when he said that Red Duke wasn't in Copper Lady's class, because he isn't. She can beat him by three lengths."

"That's good enough for me," Simms said. "I'll go back and talk to him."

Gus Van Derhoff finished his long conference with

Jimmy and walked over to Alf Frisbee.

"Well, are you game for a third?" he asked.

"Aren't you getting kind of tired of being beaten?" Alf Frisbee asked in a loud voice.

"I figure maybe I'll win some of these times," Gus replied, trying to be good-natured.

"Maybe you figure Red Duke's got more endurance even if he hasn't got half the speed," Alf said, drawing a laugh from the crowd.

"Well, do you want to try a third time or not?" Gus asked.

"Well, it's not my horse, you know," Alf Frisbee replied. "I'll have to speak to the owner."

"It's all right with me," Stephen heard Simms say. "I guess racing three quarters of a mile won't wear her out."

"Of course, this is a lot of fuss and bother just for fifty dollars," Alf Frisbee said grandly.

"Would you like to raise the ante?" Gus asked, a dangerous note in his voice.

"I would," Alf replied. "Quite a bit. I think that horse of yours should be drawing a plow."

The talkative crowd quieted, realizing that suddenly this was no longer a horse race in which fifty dollars would change hands. It was a duel between Alf Frisbee and Gus Van Derhoff. In some mysterious manner the knowledge swept through the crowd that the mood had changed, that no longer were two men making good-natured wagers. Now two gamblers playing for high stakes were facing each other. Stephen could feel a wave of tense excitement ripple through the group of onlookers, like the warning breeze before a thundershower.

"How would you like to bet the Frisbee farm?" Alf asked slowly.

There was a long silence and when Gus Van Derhoff made no reply, Alf Frisbee said, "You won it from me on a horse race. Are you going to give me a chance to get it back?"

"The Frisbee farm against what?" Gus Van Derhoff asked in low, level tones.

"Against my livery stable and everything in it," Alf Frisbee replied.

"You'll be broke if I win," Gus said, looking steadily at Alf.

"I've always managed to take care of myself," Alf replied.

Gus Van Derhoff said nothing but stuck out his big hand. They shook hands, and a long sigh swept over the crowd.

Somehow the news reached the big horseshoe of Fourth-of-July celebrants and it spread like wildfire. While before, those watching the race had been chiefly men and older boys, now men, women, and small children came pouring toward the road. Operators closed up their stands, the rides were suddenly vacated, and the celebration came to a grinding stop. The crowd by the roadside swelled until people were standing five deep at the finish line. As Stephen rode toward the starting line, he saw a woman in a blue dress come from between two stands and start hurrying toward the road.

"Aunt Hannah's heading this way," he warned Alf as he received his last-minute instructions.

"Nothing's going to stop me now," Alf said with a grin. "I'm depending on you, Steve. Ride her with a loose rein. Let her have her head and get everything out of her you can."

Stephen forgot about Hannah, about the crowd, and about everything else as he rode Copper Lady into position at the starting line for this last and all-important race. He was supremely confident that Copper Lady could win. If he could keep from making any mistakes, Copper Lady would do the rest.

Copper Lady, too, seemed to understand how much depended upon her. She pranced and danced nervously, and Stephen had to coax her into position. Once there, however, she settled down and he was able to relax his reins. He crouched low over her neck and murmured into her ear, "This is it, Lady. Give it everything you've got."

This time when the starter's flag went down, Copper Lady and Red Duke were away together, neck and neck, as though both had been fired from one gun. Stephen slackened his reins even further and dug into his mount's sides with his heels. Nothing further was needed. The copper-colored mare stretched out and ran as she had never run before. As Stephen had said to Simms, Red Duke was not in her class. By the time she reached the halfway mark, she was fully three lengths ahead and she was still gaining. A roar went up from the crowd which Copper Lady seemed to hear and appreciate, for she extended herself even further. Her hoofs beat against the dirt road in such a rapid tattoo that they seemed like a steady drumming. Almost before Stephen realized the race was well under way, she flashed across the finish line fully five lengths ahead of Red Duke.

It took another quarter of a mile to bring her back to a walk and turn her around. Stephen patted her neck and talked to her. "You're the most wonderful horse in the world, Copper Lady," he told her enthusiastically. "There's only one thing wrong with you, and that is that you don't belong to me."

Chapter VII

Gypsies

ALF FRISBEE was the happiest man in Black Hawk. The entire Frisbee livery stable was filled with amiability, good humor, and high spirits. The general feeling of contentment and happiness flowed outward from the office in a constant stream to all corners of the big building. The two jackasses added a special exuberant note to their braying, and even Gloomy Gillespie, the one bad-tempered horse in the stable, gave Stephen a friendly neigh the day following the race.

The long wooden bench, which was a fixture of the office during the winter, had long since been moved out into the street. It was filled with its usual quota of livery-stable loafers, and additional well-wishers stood around in groups discussing the race in detail. Alf Frisbee passed out cigars and chewing tobacco, and acted as master of ceremonies at the festivities.

The race was the town's one topic of conversation. Stephen found himself famous overnight. Everyone seemed happy at Alf Frisbee's triumph except Hannah and Gus Van Derhoff.

Hannah, as Stephen learned later, had created quite a scene at the celebration. The news that Alf Frisbee had bet his livery stable against the Frisbee farm had reached her where she was working in the Ladies' Aid stand. She had left immediately, determined to stop her husband from such folly. When Stephen glimpsed her, she was hurrying toward the road, breathing fire and brimstone that boded ill for everyone concerned. She had arrived at the starting line too late to stop the race but in time to berate everyone. She had screamed and shouted in her fury and called upon the forces of righteousness to punish such sinful gamblers. However, she was speaking to an unusually difficult audience. Everyone was shouting and cheering for his particular horse and Hannah's fiery tirade went almost unnoticed. As the group near the starting line hurried toward the other end of the course, she found herself not only unheard but alone. It was not until later that anyone remembered that she had tried to interfere.

"Hannah is in a right difficult position," Herb Bainbridge chuckled the following day. "She hates gambling, but she loves money. She tried to stop Alf from betting, but you know as well as I do that she's mighty happy that he won that farm back. I don't see that she can do much except keep her mouth shut. She's in what might be called an embarrassing predicament."

Hannah Frisbee did exactly that. She kept her lips tightly

closed. She maintained complete silence about the race, but it was an icy silence. She had nothing to say either to her husband or to Stephen.

Mealtime became even more of a trial to Stephen than before. Hannah continued to cook meals for them, as she considered that her wifely duty. However, she placed the dishes on the table as though she were a Christian martyr being forced to serve other Christians to the lions. Then she sat down and maintained complete silence throughout the entire meal. She picked at her food suspiciously and ate sparingly, as though it were tainted with poison. Stephen half-suspected that it was, since she bore such a grudge against Alf and himself. Now and then she would look up and glare at Alf balefully. She was not playing the part of a long-suffering martyr but waiting her turn for revenge.

Alf Frisbee refused to let his spirits be dampened by Hannah's disapproval. He seemed much less concerned than Stephen by her attitude.

"Do you suppose she's always going to stay mad at us?" Stephen asked in a worried voice.

"Don't let it worry you, Steve," Alf Frisbee assured him. "I've had what you might call long and bitter experience. Things blow over in time. Hannah's really mighty pleased that I got that farm back, only she won't admit it 'cause it won't square with her beliefs."

The day after the celebration Simms had beckoned to Stephen and, with an air of mystery, led him toward the back of the stable. He looked around carefully, examined the empty stalls, and then led Stephen to a secluded corner beside one of the feed bins.

"Things have been in such an uproar that I haven't had a chance to talk to you, Steve. I want to tell you that you did a wonderful job riding Copper Lady yesterday and I appreciate it. I owe you a lot."

"What for?" Stephen asked.

"For the simple reason that I won a pretty big sum of money myself," Simms replied.

"You did?"

"Yup, over a thousand dollars," Simms said triumphantly.

Stephen gave a long whistle. "That's wonderful! I didn't know you'd placed any bets. Who'd you win it from?"

"From about eight or nine different men," Simms replied. "Ordinarily I'm not a betting man and if it had been Alf Frisbee alone who was so certain that Copper Lady would win, I'd have kept my money in my pocket. But you had so much faith in her, too. I took every cent I had with me out to the celebration yesterday and when you said you were certain you could win that third race, I plunged."

Stephen drew a deep sigh. "I'm certainly glad I did win. I'd have let everybody I know down if I hadn't."

"I'm not much to talk about my winnings like Alf is," Simms observed. "In fact, I don't guess I ever had any before worth talking about, so unless those fellows that I bet with get together and add things up, I'd just as soon keep quiet about how much I won."

"I won't say a word," Stephen promised.

"I wanted you to know because I figure I'm in debt to you. If ever I can help you in any way, just let me know."

Half an hour later Simms appeared at the rear door of the stable and called to Stephen, who was painting a buggy out back.

"Dr. Kirk wants to know if you'll make his calls with him."

"I'm half through painting these buggy wheels," Stephen said. "I ought to finish."

"I'll finish them," Simms volunteered.

Stephen had driven with Dr. Kirk a number of times since his first trip and he knew the elderly doctor's routine well. The doctor alternated between calls on people who were actual patients and visits to old friends. Today was an unusually social day. Dr. Kirk called on three patients but stopped at five different farms to drink lemonade or eat watermelon. On their last call they stopped to check on Caleb Applegate's rheumatism and to drink buttermilk under the big elm tree in the side yard.

Caleb was in a talkative mood. "My cousin Jim Bratton died last week," he informed them. "Sudden like. Did you know Jim?"

"I don't think I did," Dr. Kirk replied. "Did he live around here long?"

"My folks raised him," Caleb replied. "But I guess he left shortly before you took up practice in Black Hawk. Jim was a few years older than me. He was mean and always picking on me. One day when he was about eighteen he just up and ran away, and I can't say that I was sorry to see him go."

"Then I gather that you don't feel any great loss at his death," Dr. Kirk observed.

Caleb Applegate chuckled. "No, but Jim was true to form. He pulled a trick just as he was dying that makes me feel like two cents."

"What was that?"

"He left me everything he had. He's visited us now and again in the last twenty or thirty years. While Martha and I were always hospitable enough, we weren't just yearning to have him stay around too long. Now he leaves me all his property. Makes me feel pretty mean."

Dr. Kirk laughed. "I wouldn't let it bother me. He probably wasn't being particularly kind or thoughtful. You may be the only relative he has."

"I guess I am," Caleb replied. "Anyhow, he left me a small farm and a threshing rig."

"That's nice," Dr. Kirk commented.

"The farm's no problem," Caleb observed. "It's rented and I can keep on renting it or I can sell it. I don't know what to do with the threshing rig, though."

"Why don't you sell it, too?" Dr. Kirk asked.

"That ain't so easy," Caleb said. "Jim ran it himself. He never married and he's either been threshing, running a sawmill, or doing something like that since he was a kid.

Here I am, the owner of a steam engine and a threshing machine, it's almost threshing time, there's a whole bunch of farmers depending on that rig, and I haven't the slightest idea what to do about it."

"I know a man who will buy it, and he can run it, too," Stephen said excitedly.

"Who?" Caleb asked.

"Simms who works in my Uncle Alf's livery stable," Stephen replied. "He ran a steam engine on a threshing circuit for several years and I know he wants to buy one."

"Has he got any money?" Caleb asked.

"He must have some," Stephen replied cautiously. "He never spends very much."

"Even if he saved it all, he probably wouldn't get rich working in a livery stable," Dr. Kirk observed.

"Well, send him out," Caleb said. "If he's got a reasonable down payment, I'm willing to talk business."

On their way back to Black Hawk Dr. Kirk looked down at Stephen's foot and said suddenly, "How long has your foot been like that, Stephen?"

"Since I was born," Stephen replied.

"Pull over to the side of the road for a minute," Dr. Kirk directed.

Stephen pulled on the reins and stopped the horses at one side of the road.

"Take off your shoe and let me look at it," Dr. Kirk told him.

Silently, Stephen removed his shoe and held his deformed foot out for Dr. Kirk to examine. He had no objection to talking to people like doctors about his foot because they didn't act as if he were a freak or something abnormal.

Dr. Kirk looked at the twisted foot carefully, feeling it here and there, and asking Stephen to bend his ankle this way and that.

"Put your shoe back on," he said finally, picking up the reins. He drove on in silence until Stephen had replaced his sock and laced up his shoe.

"That should have been treated when you were much younger," he said. "However, one leg is not longer than the other, which is the important thing."

"Do you think anything can be done with it?" Stephen asked eagerly.

"I'm not a specialist and I couldn't say for certain," Dr. Kirk replied. "Offhand, I'd say there was a good chance. You'd probably have to wear braces on it for several years. You might even have to have an operation or two, but a a good foot man could probably straighten it out."

Simms was very interested in the news about Caleb Applegate's threshing rig, as Stephen had expected. He immediately went to Alf Frisbee and asked for the remainder of the day off. Copper Lady had been turned into the pasture that Alf Frisbee rented for his extra horses, for everyone felt that she deserved a few days in which to romp and run as she chose. Simms borrowed another horse, threw a saddle on its back, and rode off to see Caleb

Applegate. He was gone for several hours, and when he returned his eyes were gleaming with excitement.

"I think I've bought me a threshing rig," he told Stephen happily. "Naturally, I want to see it first, but if it's a Case machine and only five or six years old, as Applegate says it is, and unless it's received some mighty hard treatment, I think I'm getting a real bargain."

"When are you going to see it?" Stephen asked.

"I'm going to catch that train out at four o'clock in the morning if it's all right with Alf," Simms replied. "My leaving sudden this way will sort of put him in a hole."

Alf Frisbee, however, was all encouragement. "I certainly wouldn't stand in your way if you have a good opportunity," he said heartily. "When a man gets a chance like that, he has to grab it. Steve and I will take care of the stable until we find someone. Things will probably be slow for the next two weeks, anyhow. Naturally, I'm going to miss you, but we'll get along."

Stephen knew, however, that he would be the one who would really miss Simms. The tall, lanky man with the hideous purple birthmark had become a valued friend. Simms had no interesting gossip to relate as did Herb Bainbridge, he knew no funny jokes, he told no wild tales, and only on rare occasions did he talk about his past. Nevertheless, he was an excellent companion. In many ways Simms and Stephen were alike—they were both reserved, quiet, and somewhat shy. They worked together in quiet understanding. Simms seldom gave Stephen any orders because orders were seldom necessary. Stephen could sense from the older man's actions what he was supposed to do when they were working together on a job. Now that Simms was leaving so abruptly, Stephen suddenly awoke to the fact that he was losing the closest friend he had ever known. Stephen believed in keeping his troubles to himself, but what confiding he had done had been to Simms. Since that day in the carriage shed, when Simms had found him crying, there had been a bond of understanding between them.

"I'm glad you're getting a chance to buy a threshing rig, but I'm going to be sorry to see you go," he told Simms honestly.

Simms shifted awkwardly from one foot to the other. "I know what you mean, and I feel the same way. But I'll be back after threshing season's over. You can depend on it."

"What about Copper Lady?" Stephen asked, suddenly remembering Simms's horse.

"I'm going to leave her here for the time being," Simms said.

"Then I know you'll be back," Stephen said with relief. "You couldn't leave her."

Just before he went to bed that night he went back to the stable and said good-by to Simms. Then, feeling rather sad and lonely, he returned to his room and climbed into bed. Hannah would be glad, he thought, as he lay awake in the dark room. Simms was a drifter, a foreigner, who did not belong in Black Hawk as far as she was concerned.

Stephen was uncertain whether he wanted Simms to come back soon or late to get Copper Lady. Once the horse was gone, Stephen would probably never see her again. He would no longer be able to race up and down the countryside. Perhaps a miracle would occur, though. Simms might bring his threshing rig back with him, and next year thresh for farmers near Black Hawk. Then perhaps he would keep Copper Lady at the Frisbee livery stables and Steve could continue to exercise her. He might even get a job with Simms on the threshing rig. He pictured himself riding out to a nearby farm as threshing operations started, while all the threshers with their heavy work teams paused to gaze in admiration at Copper Lady. Then another thought caused his rosy dreams to vanish. As Hannah had so bitingly remarked, wishes were not horses, and never would be.

Two days after Simms's departure Alf Frisbee accomplished a minor miracle by persuading Herb Bainbridge to work for several days. Then early the following morning he harnessed up a team and set out for Herkimer City, the county seat, some twenty miles away.

"I'm to meet Gus Van Derhoff at the lawyer's, and we're going to transfer the farm," he told Hannah and Steve at breakfast. "I want to get the deed recorded and everything all finished, and I imagine it'll take most of the day. I need a couple of new sets of harness. Maybe I can pick up a buggy, and there are some other things I might just as well get while I'm there. I'll stay the night and I should be back some time late tomorrow afternoon or evening."

For the first time in five days Hannah came out of her exile to speak.

"Who's looking after the livery stable?" she asked in a hard voice.

"Herb Bainbridge and Steve here," Alf replied, busily eating his eggs and bacon.

"Humph," said Hannah scornfully. "Of all the no-accounts in town, why did you have to hire the worst?"

"He's the only man I could get," Alf Frisbee replied. "Besides, Herb is reliable enough. It's just that he won't overwork himself."

"I'd feel a lot better if Simms were here," Hannah remarked. "Herb Bainbridge wouldn't stir himself if the building caught on fire."

"I thought you didn't like Simms," Alf said with an amused glance at Steve. "You said he was a drifter and didn't belong here. That's why I didn't put up any objection when he left so sudden like."

Hannah glared at her husband with her dark eyes snapping. Alf had been acting much too independent since he had won the race, and she was worried that she would lose control. She looked down at her plate and then said with unusual mildness, "I'll drop by the stable now and then to see that things are going all right."

"That'd be fine," Alf said, looking at his wife in surprise.

Wednesday, the day that Alf left, was unusually quiet. By noon they had only one team out for hire. Even though Stephen did all the work by himself, the usual tasks were finished by ten o'clock and he and Herb Bainbridge spent the remainder of the morning sitting on the bench in front of the stable. Herb was a true executive. He enjoyed making decisions and issuing orders if someone else did the work. Stephen did not mind the work if he could keep up with it, and Herb was amusing and interesting company.

They took turns going to lunch. Both had returned when Hannah suddenly appeared, entering through the back door of the stable. Her face was flushed with excitement.

"Gypsies are coming!" she said. "They're only a mile south of town right now. I just had a phone call from Mrs. Campbell. Stephen, you go up and down both sides of the street and tell all the merchants. Herb, you'd better close the doors to the stable."

Herb made a sour face and got slowly to his feet. Stephen stood by the bench indecisively.

"Well, go on," Hannah said testily. "What are you waiting for?"

"What should I tell them?" Stephen asked.

"Just what I said," Hannah replied, "that the gypsies are coming. They'll be here in another five or ten minutes. Land sakes alive, Stephen, haven't you ever seen gypsies descend on a town?"

"No, I haven't."

"Well, they'll steal you blind. They go into every store

by the dozens, and the women and children pick up anything they can get their fingers on. Those gypsy women
with their great big skirts can hide almost anything.
They've even been known to steal little children."

Stephen waited no longer. He went scurrying up the
street. He entered the grocery store, the drugstore, the
harness maker's, and each establishment in turn, telling the
proprietor the news. Some acted as excited as Hannah and
immediately began closing their doors. Others merely
nodded and thanked Stephen for telling them but made
no other move. Stephen took advantage of his position as
messenger to enter one of the pool halls. That had been
strictly forbidden territory and he had never been in the
building before. He told Rommey, the proprietor, about
the gypsies, and then glanced guiltily around the big
gloomy interior. There was a long bar and back of that six
pool tables. Only one was in use, and Stephen recognized
both of the players. They often loafed at the livery stable.
He was disappointed. There were no desperate drunken
characters loafing around and he failed to see what was so
sinful about a green pool table. He decided to ask Herb
Bainbridge about it later and hurried on down the street to
warn the other merchants in town.

When he returned to the stables, the big double doors
were closed as well as the smaller door leading into the
office. Herb was once more seated on his bench, calmly
surveying the peaceful business district of Black Hawk.

"Hannah went on to tell her neighbors," Herb observed

dryly. "There's nothing that woman loves more than an exciting piece of news, lessen it's an argument."

"What are these gypsies like?" Stephen asked.

"Just like you and me," Herb Bainbridge said. "They've got a dark skin and the women dress in big bright-colored skirts and they wear earrings in their ears. Otherwise they're pretty much the same as anybody else."

"Why is Hannah so scared of them," Stephen asked, "and a lot of other people, too? Half the places in town are closed up."

Herb Bainbridge spat tobacco juice accurately at a fly, drowning it in the brown fluid.

"Most people are fools," he said contemptuously. "Mainly, gypsies are horse traders, and when it comes to trading or buying horses they're sharp dealers. They know a lot about horses, too. They can take a sick old nag and in a few weeks make him look like a young, healthy horse. I s'pose they've learned a lot about horse doctoring and passed it on from father to son. Anyhow, watch your step if you ever trade horses with a gypsy, although I've known farmers who have bought horses or traded horses with gypsies and claimed they got wonderful teams."

"Where do they live?" Stephen asked.

"In wagons," Herb Bainbridge replied. "They travel around the country in bands of maybe eight, ten, or twelve wagons, each one with a string of horses. There's always a leader or a king, as they call him, who seems to run the group. They camp out nights sleeping on the ground if it's clear, and in their wagons if it rains. Sometimes they put up tents."

"What do they do in wintertime?" Stephen asked.

"That I don't rightly know," Herb replied. "I suppose they go South someplace and do the same thing."

"You mean they live just trading horses?" Stephen asked.

"Mainly that," Herb replied. "One thing a gypsy won't do and that's a day's work. He doesn't see any need to." Herb grinned at Stephen. "Maybe I'm part gypsy myself."

"I guess they have to be sharp horse traders if that's all they do," Stephen observed.

"Oh, they do other things, too," Herb said. "They'll trade most anything, and the women go around telling fortunes. For fifty cents they'll read your palm and tell you what your future is."

"I'd like to have mine read," Stephen said.

"Don't let Hannah catch you at it," Herb warned. "I remember one day about five years ago a gypsy woman was reading Alf's palm right here in front of the livery stable and Hannah came walking down the street. It had been raining, and she had her umbrella in her hand. When she saw this gypsy woman telling Alf's fortune, she saw red. She took after her with the umbrella and beat the poor woman all the way to the next corner."

"I guess maybe I won't have my fortune told," Steve said with a slight smile.

"Now some folks, like Hannah, claim that gypsies steal. Maybe they do, I don't know. I know that a lot of merchants complain that things disappear after gypsies have been in town, but it would be my guess that the gypsies get blamed for a lot of things that they don't do. There are probably thieves among them, just like I know a few thieves right here in Black Hawk. But as for their stealing little children, that's a lot of nonsense. Gypsies are pretty smart people. They got more kids of their own than they know what to do with, why should they steal more?"

Hannah returned and entered the office, where she sat in Alf's chair before the roll-top desk, her lips compressed in a straight, hard line as though ready to give her life to defend her property. A few minutes later the gypsies came into view at the other end of the long street. In spite of Herb Bainbridge's information, Stephen was unprepared for what he saw. They were not driving the common grain or lumber wagons that the Iowa farmers used. The gypsy wagons were high, enclosed vehicles with a roof, windows in the sides, and a high seat up front. Most of them were painted in bright colors and closely resembled circus wagons that Stephen had seen in Chicago. Seated in the driver's seat was a man or a boy, and beside him in most cases was a gypsy woman in a huge, brightly colored flowing skirt. Both men and women wore bright dangling earrings. Most of the men were hatless, while the women had brightly colored kerchiefs tied over their jet-black hair. Peering out of the windows and the back ends of the wagons were dozens of small swarthy faces. Herb Bainbridge had spoken the truth. The gypsies had children enough of their own.

Following each wagon was a string of at least a dozen horses. Stephen had never seen so many horses at one time and one place in his life. There were roans, bays, grays, pintos, white horses, black horses, spotted horses, buckskins, and oddly mottled and dappled horses of all shades and colors. They were big, little, and medium. Some were fat and frisky while others looked bony and dejected. At the end of one string trotted two mules and a donkey.

Every gypsy child more than five or six years of age was an expert horseman and was riding. Most of them rode without saddles and with the most makeshift bridles Stephen had ever seen. They were perfectly at ease on their mounts, however, and they rode through town gazing curiously about with their dark, gentle eyes.

Dan Gerber, who ran the barbershop several doors from the livery stable and did double duty as Black Hawk's constable when required, stood at the intersection between Black Hawk's two business blocks—his silver star pinned conspicuously to his shirt—frowning at the gypsies as they passed through town. One gypsy with a hawklike nose and curly black hair handed the reins of his horses to his wife and jumped lithely from the moving wagon. He walked across the dusty street and spoke to Dan Gerber for a few minutes. Dan Gerber listened and then nodded solemnly in return.

The caravan continued on to the next corner, where it

turned right toward Black Hawk's so-called city park. This was an entire square block usually overgrown with weeds except on the two or three occasions when the city council voted sufficient funds to have it mowed. A large hitching lot and watering trough were located at the far end of the park. The first gypsy wagon turned into this and soon the park overflowed with gypsies. It was busier than it had been for years. Dan Gerber, after the last gypsy had left the business section, started down the street toward his barbershop.

"I told them they could rest an hour or so in the park," he told the curious townspeople who stopped him on the way. "After all, until they've broken the law, you can't very well chase them out of town."

Hannah Frisbee had left her position at the desk and was standing in the door of the office. "Humph!" she said when she heard Dan Gerber's remarks. "I can't see any reason why they should use the city park. They don't pay taxes."

It seemed the gypsies scarcely had driven out of sight when they reappeared. They descended upon the business section like a flock of migrating birds. Steve rubbed his eyes and stared at them in disbelief. How so many could have been in that one short wagon train baffled him. The men and older boys strolled indolently up and down the streets, some of them entering the cafés or grocery stores to make small purchases. While the men seemed to be enjoying a lazy visit, the women were incredibly busy. Young and old, they went up and down the streets, in and out of every store that was open, and after each woman tagged at least three or four small children. Black Hawk was suddenly vibrating with life. The women's volum- inous, swirling skirts were of reds, yellows, blues, pinks, and all colors of the rainbow. In spite of the heat some of the older women wore colorful shawls around their shoulders.

Stephen watched with interest. A lithe young gypsy woman came walking toward the bench where he and

Herb Bainbridge sat. Steve contrasted her smooth dark face and large brown eyes with Hannah's cold, pinched countenance.

"Tell your fortune?" the gypsy woman asked in a low, husky voice.

"No, get out!" Hannah ordered coldly.

The gypsy woman appeared not to have heard her but repeated her question to Herb Bainbridge.

"I can read your future from your palm," she urged.

Herb Bainbridge chuckled. "No, I guess not," he said kindly. "I guess I pretty well know my future. It's dedicated to keeping any blisters from growing on my palms."

The gypsy nodded and tossed a fleeting smile at Stephen, pointedly ignored Hannah, and passed on down the street.

"Right pretty gal," Herb Bainbridge commented.

"Humph!" snorted Hannah. "I'll bet she hasn't had a bath in six months." She turned and went back to her seat at the desk.

Most of the gypsies had returned to the city park when the tall man who had talked to Dan Gerber suddenly appeared at Herb Bainbridge's elbow. He glanced up at the sign above them.

"Are you Mr. Frisbee?" he asked Bainbridge.

"Nope," Herb replied. "He ain't here. Why?"

"I would like to trade horses."

Herb scratched his ear. "Well, Mrs. Frisbee's inside in the office," he said with a slight smile. "Maybe she'd like to swap a few horses." He winked at Stephen.

The bareheaded gypsy thanked Herb gravely and stepped through the open office door. He caught Hannah by surprise and she jumped up from her seat at the desk in alarm. The gypsy bowed and flashed her a smile which showed two rows of even white teeth.

"You are Mrs. Frisbee?" he asked politely.

Hannah said nothing but gave him a nod, indicating that he was right.

"I would like to trade horses," he continued.

"My husband is away," Hannah said coldly.

The gypsy shrugged slightly. "Then aren't you in charge while he's away?" he asked.

Hannah drew herself erect.

"I am in charge," she said coldly, "but I don't care to trade horses with you."

He made no reply but bowed, turned gracefully, and walked back through the door. He had gone perhaps twenty feet when suddenly Hannah appeared.

"Wait just a moment," she called.

She hurried after him while he waited with one dark eyebrow raised quizzically.

When she reached the waiting gypsy she stood with her back toward Herb Bainbridge and Steve, and talked to the tall, dark man for several minutes. He listened intently, made several comments, and then nodded twice. Hannah returned and without a word of explanation went back into the office. A few minutes later the gypsy caravan appeared again, headed toward the next small town of

Blairsburg. Stephen walked to the corner and watched them until they were out of sight. Several gypsy boys, perhaps two or three years his junior, brought up the rear. They were riding sleek-looking horses and seemed to be playing some sort of horseback game which they enjoyed immensely.

As yet no one had accused the departing band of stealing anything, and from what Stephen had seen, they had been very well behaved. Whatever their faults they seemed to be kind to each other and their children appeared happy. Stephen gazed after them almost enviously.

Alf Frisbee did not lock the big stable doors on hot summer nights. Instead, he locked the individual doors to the tack room, the office, and feed room. Someone was usually on duty until approximately nine o'clock, so after supper Stephen hurried back to the stable. He much preferred the atmosphere there to that of the silent, hostile house. Meals with Hannah were bad enough. He had no desire to sit with her in the parlor while she rocked back and forth, repeating gossip to him about people whom he did not know.

The evening passed quietly, and before Stephen realized it, it was almost nine-thirty. Locking up was not too strenuous for Herb Bainbridge so he helped Stephen get the big barn in readiness for the night. They tossed some hay to the few horses that needed it and turned out the lanterns. After saying good night to Herb, Stephen went out the back way and across the alley to the little gray house. Hannah was in her usual chair in the living room.

He said good night to her, too, and went upstairs to bed.

The day had been still and hot and there was no hint of an evening breeze. Stephen's low-ceilinged room was almost unbearably hot. After tossing and turning for an hour, he decided to go out to the pump for a drink of fresh water. He slipped on his trousers and went downstairs. All the lights in the house were out and he assumed that Hannah was asleep. Quietly he opened the kitchen door and slipped into the back yard. As he did so, he saw a shadow cross the alley near the stable. He watched but it did not reappear. He tried to convince himself that he had seen nothing, and that the safe and sensible thing to do was to get his drink of water and return to bed. Then he faced the truth—he was afraid to investigate. He clamped his teeth together, squared his shoulders, and started toward the stable, walking as quietly as possible.

There was a sliver of a moon which cast a dim light. Staying in the protective shadow of various bushes, trees, and buildings, Stephen made his way to the stable. He felt reasonably certain that anyone there had not seen him. Slowly and cautiously he inched forward until he was standing within a few feet of the open rear entrance. Then he heard voices, and there was no mistaking one of them. It belonged to Hannah Frisbee.

"That's not enough," she said decisively.

"I will pay you three hundred dollars," a soft male voice answered. "That's as high as I will go."

"Have you got the money with you?" Hannah asked.

"In my pocket," the man replied. "If you will light a light you can count it."

"Never mind, I think there will be enough light here in the door," Hannah said.

Stephen shrank back flat against the wall and watched while Hannah appeared in the rear door, her head bent down over something in her hands. She stood that way for several minutes, her back half-turned toward him, and then she once more disappeared inside the building.

"It's three hundred dollars," she announced.

She had apparently moved further away from the door because the conversation became indistinct. Then, suddenly, a tall figure appeared and walked with catlike grace out into the alley. Stephen looked at the dim figure for a minute and realized that it was one of the gypsies. So Hannah had decided to trade or sell some horses after all. But why was she so secretive about it? He suspected that Alf was not going to like whatever bargain she had made. However, it was not his business and he had no intention of saying anything.

He stood where he was, waiting for Hannah. After a few minutes she appeared and he watched while she crossed the alley and entered the back door of the house. It would probably be half an hour before he could hope to enter the house undetected. Anyhow, he was hot and thirsty and did not feel like sleeping. He went through the stable and walked slowly down the street toward the depot. There was a pump just outside the station. He would get a drink there.

Chapter VIII

The Stolen Horse

ALF FRISBEE returned late the next evening with a
new buggy, several sets of harness, and a number
of packages containing new clothes for Stephen.
He also had several presents for Hannah which
he offered in what was an obvious bid for peace. Hannah
accepted the gifts with surprising cordiality. In fact, she
had been in good humor all day, but Alf, not knowing
this, decided that his gifts had worked a miracle.

"A man forgets what he knew in his courting days," he
told Stephen later in the stable. "You can buy a woman a
few trinkets, a new hat, or some sort of a present, and she's
pleased as can be. A woman'll forgive almost anything
if you show her a little attention."

Stephen wasn't quite sure what Hannah was supposed
to be forgiving, but he said nothing.

The next day Stephen drove the Methodist minister
around the surrounding countryside for several hours while
the minister made calls connected with the church. He

returned just before noon to find that Alf Frisbee had again departed for the county seat.

"He went after the sheriff," Herb Bainbridge said. "I never saw a man in such a rage. Copper Lady has disappeared!"

"Disappeared?" Steve asked.

"Well, Alf says she's stolen," Herb replied. "He doesn't know for sure, but he went after the sheriff anyhow."

"Tell me about it," Stephen urged.

"There isn't much to tell," Herb replied. "Alf went out to the pasture that he rents about ten o'clock, planning to switch a team here in the barn for one that he had out there. When he got there, he counted horses naturally, and Copper Lady wasn't there. Harvey Edinminster owns that land, you know, so Alf went to see him. Harvey couldn't tell him a thing. He can see the pasture from the kitchen window, but of course he doesn't spend his time sitting there counting horses. Then, as Alf was leaving, Edinminster's hired hand came in, and he claimed he saw one of the gypsies looking at the horses a couple of days before. That would be the day they were here in town. Alf got all excited, figuring that maybe the gypsies stole her. He came back here in a lather, saddled up that big black horse, and took off for the county seat in a cloud of dust."

"Were there any other horses missing?" Stephen asked.

"If there were, he didn't mention them."

"Do you think they'll find the gypsies?"

"Maybe, and maybe not," Herb replied. "But if they do,

I bet they won't find Copper Lady. I can see why the
gypsies would want her. They really appreciate good
horses and they would have to go a long ways to find one
her equal. I doubt if they would be dumb enough to steal
her and then mosey along with her in the regular caravan
waiting for the sheriff to catch up."

Stephen was worried and upset both because Copper
Lady was gone and because he suspected that the trouble
over her disappearance was just beginning. When he went
home to lunch, he told the news to Hannah. He watched
her closely but she did not seem at all disturbed.

"It's a good riddance," she said calmly. "Now both that
drifter and his horse are gone and I'm glad of it."

"But she's a valuable horse," Stephen protested.

"Then Simms shouldn't have left her here for Alf to
care for," Hannah said righteously. "After all, what does
he expect Alf to do, stand out there and guard her with a
gun? If she's so valuable, he should look after her himself."

Her attitude puzzled Stephen. If she had sold Copper
Lady to the gypsies, as Stephen suspected, she was acting
surprisingly unconcerned. "Do you think they'll catch the
gypsies?" he asked.

"It's not likely," Hannah said. "There's no telling where
those heathens go when they leave a town."

Perhaps she was right, but still there was always the possibility they could be traced. Hannah must have made some
plans or provision for such an event. Stephen decided that
there was little he could do but keep silent and pray that
Copper Lady would be returned somehow. On his way

back to the stable he detoured to go by the post office.

"Mr. Pierce, did Bob Simms leave any forwarding address with you when he left a few days ago?" he asked the postmaster.

"Nope, but he's over somewhere near Pitman because his postcard was mailed there. That's over south of Marshalltown."

"What postcard?" Stephen asked.

"The one he sent you," Pierce replied. "Just came in the afternoon mail yesterday. I guess I haven't given it to you yet. I put it with your Uncle Alf's mail and he hasn't picked it up today."

He reached up and pulled a postcard from a cubbyhole and handed it to Stephen. As he had said, it was postmarked Pitman, Iowa, and dated two days before. On the front of the card was a picture of a 1909 Model 30 Cadillac with its proud owner standing beside it in a long linen duster. On the other side, in a surprisingly neat hand, Simms had written, "Dear Steve, I bought the threshing rig. Got a good deal, thanks to you. Crops are early and I should start threshing next week. See you this fall. Take care of yourself. Bob Simms." There was no return address.

Stephen tucked the postcard in his pocket and went back to the stable. Herb Bainbridge had good news.

"Well, I had a call from your uncle," he announced. "He has the horse and he has the man who took her."

"I'm glad that he got Copper Lady back," Stephen said thankfully. "Who stole her?"

"One of the gypsies," Herb Bainbridge replied. "I guess

I was wrong. There the horse was, trotting along with a string, big as life. Gypsies must not be as foxy as I thought they were."

"When will Uncle Alf be back?" Stephen asked.

"He's on his way back now," Herb replied. "He should be here some time this evening. He said to tell Hannah he'd be home for supper but would be late. You know, there's something peculiar about that."

"About what?"

"The sheriff is coming back here with him and bringing the gypsy along. Now why would he want to do that? Black Hawk's way out of his way. The jail is over in the county seat."

"I guess I'd better go tell Aunt Hannah," Stephen said, deciding that the sheriff's actions were not his problem.

Hannah, however, was not at home when Stephen reached the house. As she might be visiting any of half-a-dozen friends, Stephen made no attempt to find her but returned to the stable. He and Herb Bainbridge spent a busy afternoon. Everyone wanted a buggy and team at once. About three o'clock Mrs. Grover asked for a rig and someone to drive her several miles out in the country to see a sick friend. Since Stephen was the only one available, he received the job. It was almost six o'clock when he returned. Herb Bainbridge had been alone during his absence and naturally had done as little as possible. There was no hay in the mangers, several sets of harness were damp with perspiration and needed cleaning, and all the horses had to be fed their grain. In the rush of doing this, Stephen forgot all about Hannah. When he looked at the clock it was six-thirty, the hour when they ordinarily ate supper, and he had told her nothing about Alf's possible late return. Feeling guilty and apprehensive, he hurried to tell Herb Bainbridge that he was going to eat. He hoped that whatever Hannah had prepared for supper would keep until Alf got there. He was certain to receive a lecture anyhow, for not having delivered Alf's message more promptly. The most he could hope was that it would not be mixed with a sermon on the sin of wastefulness.

Herb Bainbridge was sitting on the bench in front of the stable and as Stephen stepped through the door to speak to him, he saw his uncle coming down the street. He was riding his black horse and behind him on a tether was Copper Lady. Alf looked tired, dusty, and out of sorts. A few feet behind him was a buggy and in it was a man in a broad-brimmed hat with a star on his blue denim shirt. Beside him sat the tall, hawk-nosed gypsy who had wanted to trade horses two days before.

Alf Frisbee dismounted stiffly at the livery-stable door, nodded to Stephen, and turned to Herb Bainbridge.

"You might as well go on and get yourself something to eat, Herb. Stephen and I will take care of things here."

"You're tired," Herb Bainbridge said. "I'm in no hurry; go ahead and eat. I'm just settin' anyhow."

"No, I'd rather you went ahead," Alf said. "The sheriff and I have got a few things to talk over."

Herb took the hint and with a slightly injured air got to his feet and walked down the street.

"Stephen, will you go over and ask your Aunt Hannah to come over for a few minutes?" Alf asked grimly.

Hannah was in the kitchen when Stephen arrived at the house. She looked at the clock and said angrily, "It's about time! I sweat and slave over the stove getting a hot meal for you and then you're late."

"Uncle Alf would like you to come over to the stable," Stephen said.

"What for?" she asked sharply.

"I don't know," Stephen said truthfully. "He just came back with Copper Lady. The sheriff's with him, and also a gypsy."

Hannah's face took on a sudden stricken look. Slowly she wiped her hands on the roller towel and took off her apron. She looked at Stephen warily and said, "What else did he say?"

"Nothing, that's all."

Ordinarily, Hannah's walk was fast and nervous, but her pace was slow and deliberate as she walked toward the stable. Stephen arrived almost a minute ahead of her. She came through the rear door of the stable. The sheriff had driven his team through the big doors, and Alf Frisbee was giving each of the horses a bucket of water. The gypsy was standing by the inner door of the office, his dark face haughty and impassive. The sheriff stood a few feet nearer the door leaning on the back end of his buggy. He had removed his hat and was mopping his red and perspiring brow. Evidently, he had had a long, hot ride in the afternoon sun and he, too, appeared out of sorts. Hannah walked up to the group and stood looking at them, stony-faced and silent.

"This is my wife," Alf Frisbee announced. "Hannah, this is Sheriff Gleason and Mr. Zorro."

The sheriff nodded but neither the gypsy nor Hannah moved a muscle of their faces to indicate that they had heard the introduction.

"Is this the woman?" Sheriff Gleason asked the gypsy.

The gypsy nodded gravely. "She is the one. Mrs. Frisbee."

The sheriff looked at Alf Frisbee, who cleared his throat and said, "Hannah, I'll come right to the point. This fellow claims you sold him Copper Lady for three hundred dollars. Did you?"

Hannah turned her head slowly and looked coldly at the waiting gypsy.

"This is the man who was here during the afternoon. He said he wanted to buy or trade horses and I told him that I wasn't interested, that you were away."

The gypsy's eyes narrowed slightly and he drew a deep breath, but otherwise he showed no emotion at her denial of his story.

"Then you didn't sell him the horse?" the sheriff asked.

Hannah did not hesitate. "Of course not," she replied. "I never saw him again."

Stephen listened to her firm, hard voice in horrified amazement. She was deliberately lying; she was going to stand by while the gypsy was jailed for stealing a horse that he had bought. Stephen looked from her cold, hard face to that of the still impassive gypsy. He could not believe anyone capable of such meanness and dishonesty.

"Well, I guess that's all I wanted to know," the sheriff said. "Come on, we've still got about twenty miles to go to the county jail."

Stephen swallowed. There was a large lump in his throat and he was afraid, but if he remained silent and allowed the sheriff to take the gypsy, he would be only one shade better than Hannah.

"She did too sell him the horse," he blurted out. "I heard them talking. He paid her three hundred dollars and I saw her count the money."

All four pairs of eyes turned to look at him. The gypsy's face showed its first sign of expression. There was a slight flicker of hope in his dark eyes. The sheriff looked startled, while Alf Frisbee stared at his wife with suppressed rage. Stephen's gaze was held by his aunt's face. She glared at him with such pure, blazing hatred that he shrank back several steps but was unable to look away.

"When did this happen?" the sheriff asked.

"Night before last, about ten o'clock," Stephen replied, wrenching his eyes away from Hannah's. "I couldn't get to sleep and I was thirsty, so I went downstairs and started toward the pump. I thought I saw a shadow over here and

I came over to investigate. I heard Aunt Hannah and a man talking inside. He offered her three hundred dollars for something. She took it and came to the back door and counted it there in the moonlight. Then I saw the man leave, and I'm certain that it was this gypsy here. A little later Aunt Hannah went back to the house."

"Then you know he bought something from her but you're not certain that it was a horse?" the sheriff asked.

By this time Alf Frisbee's face was a mottled red and he appeared in danger of choking. Finally he found his voice and asked hoarsely, "Hannah, did you sell him that horse? Tell me the truth, because if you don't, so help me, I'll beat it out of you."

Hannah lifted her head and stared at him defiantly. "All right, I sold it," she said. "I didn't want her around here. Sooner or later you'd bet on her again and lose every cent we have."

Alf took a deep breath, as though trying to contain himself. He clenched and unclenched his hands.

"Get back to the house and get the money he gave you," he said. Hannah turned, and Alf added, "And I don't want you to come back in this stable again ever. Stephen, you go with her and bring the money back."

Stephen waited in the kitchen while Hannah went into the bedroom for the money which she had secreted some place. She was gone only a minute and when she returned she threw a roll of bills on the oilcloth-covered kitchen table.

"Kith and kin mean nothing to you, do they?" she asked in a low, hard voice. "You'd take the part of that greasy gypsy against your own aunt. That's the gratitude I get for washing and ironing your clothes and cooking your meals. You're no good, Stephen McGowan, just like your mother and father before you. Don't think I'll forget this. I'll remember it until my dying day."

There was no mistaking the threat in her tone, and Stephen had no doubt of her memory or her blazing hatred. Hastily, he grabbed the roll of bills and scurried out of the house and back to the stable.

"I'm sorry for all the trouble I've caused you," Alf Frisbee told the sheriff. "I'm ashamed of the way my wife acted. I suppose I should have better control over what she does."

"It's kind of hard to control a woman sometimes," Sheriff Gleason said understandingly.

"If there are any costs, let me know," Alf said. "I'll square things up with this man here and see that he gets back to his family."

"I guess that about clears things up then," the sheriff said, climbing wearily back into his buggy.

Alf Frisbee shifted from one foot to the other. "I know it's asking a lot," he said, "but I'd appreciate it if you'd say nothing about Hannah denying that she'd sold that horse. It ain't something I'm exactly proud of."

"If anybody asks, I'll just tell them it was all a misunderstanding," the sheriff said agreeably. "She'd sold the horse and you didn't know she'd sold it."

The sheriff drove off, and Alf Frisbee turned to the silent waiting gypsy.

"I'm sorry about all the trouble I've caused you, too, and I want to apologize for accusing you of stealing a horse. My wife had no business selling that horse and you had no business buying it from her."

The gypsy shrugged. "She said she was in charge here."

"Women don't usually buy and sell horses," Alf said. "You know that as well as I do. You don't go around trading horses with farmers' wives just because their husbands happen to be away for the day."

"She said the horse was hers to sell if she wanted to," the gypsy insisted solemnly.

"But it wasn't," Stephen interrupted. "She belongs to Bob Simms. We're just keeping her here."

"Anyhow, I'm not going to allow you to take her," Alf Frisbee said firmly. "You must have known there was something wrong with the deal, sneaking back here at night to pay Hannah after dark. Here's your three hundred dollars and I'll tell you what else I'll do. You pick out another horse here in the stable, and I'll let you have her for almost anything you want to offer. You can also take off twenty dollars from the price because of the day you've lost."

The gypsy decided that the offer was better than nothing. He picked a small bay mare for which he gave Alf Frisbee fifty-five dollars. It was a rare bargain, as both he and Alf knew. Alf gave him an old bridle, and the gypsy led the horse to the door. He paused, looked gravely at Stephen, and said, "Thank you. If the gypsies can ever do you a favor, ask for Zorro." Then he leaped lightly on the back of the bay and was off down the street at a smart canter. Alf Frisbee and Stephen watched him until he disappeared, and then Alf turned to his nephew and said, "You know, I think maybe we'd better go eat dinner at the café tonight."

Chapter IX

Flight

STEPHEN had difficulty getting to sleep that night. The house had been hostile enough before, but now he knew it would be infinitely worse. Hannah did not make threats lightly and she had a long, long memory. She would be watching and waiting for her chance at revenge. She had disliked him before, and now she hated him. Her remark about washing and ironing and cooking for him troubled him. Each thing that she did for him would rankle and hurt and add fuel to the fires of her hatred.

His Uncle Alf was on his side and would do his best to protect him. But that was not enough. Alf, with his bluff heartiness, could never protect anyone against Hannah's sly scheming. She would watch and wait and Alf would not even notice the thousand-and-one little tricks she would think of.

Stephen finally drifted off to sleep, and sometime during the night he came to a decision. He would leave Black

Hawk. The decision neither frightened nor surprised him. He realized that he had known from the day of his arrival that sooner or later he would leave. This was not his home and never could be. Only a woman like his mother, with love in her heart, could make a home.

He liked his Uncle Alf and would miss him, but he would rather be completely alone in the world than living in the same house with Hannah's hatred. A few short months before, he would have been too frightened to set out by himself but now he had more confidence. He could handle horses and he had won a race. He could take care of himself.

The first few streaks of light were stealing through the eastern sky when he arose and packed. He started down the stairs and then remembered his mother's photograph. That was something else for which he blamed Hannah— she was destroying his memory of his mother. During those first few weeks in Black Hawk he had been able to call his mother's picture to mind at will. Without closing his eyes he could picture her face, her soft blue eyes, her smile, and the way her hair curled back from her white forehead. But of late the sharp image had become blurred. Hannah's dark, suspicious eyes and thin, tight lips kept forcing their way into his mind's picture. When he tried to recall his mother's warm voice, he heard Hannah's cold, hard tones. He could no longer see his mother clearly without the photograph.

In the kitchen he paused to scribble a hasty note to Alf:

Dear Uncle Alf,

I think things would be easier if I wasn't around. Don't worry about me. I'll be able to take care of myself. If I really need your help I'll get in touch with you. Thanks for putting me up as long as you have.

Steve

He placed the note on the kitchen table and then changed his mind. He picked it up, shouldered his bag, and walked across the alley, where he left the note tucked beneath the office door. Then he hurried out, anxious to be gone before it was really light.

He reached the main graveled road five miles south of Black Hawk before the farmers had finished their chores and were in the fields. He turned and trudged eastward because he knew that Pitman and Marshalltown were somewhere in that direction. For the first three or four miles each time a wagon appeared he vanished into the cornfields and waited until it had passed. By the time he had gone eight or nine miles he decided that it was unlikely anyone he knew would be in that vicinity, so he boldly continued walking down the road. Although it was still only about eight o'clock it was hot and he was growing hungry.

He was offered a ride about eight-thirty with an insurance salesman who took him on to the next small town about six miles to the east. There he ate breakfast in a café and for the first time counted his money. He had seven dollars and sixty-five cents after paying for his breakfast.

It wasn't much, but he was not worried. He was confident of his ability to handle horses if nothing else. At this season of the year almost any farmer would be willing to let him sleep in the haymow and would furnish him his meals in return for his doing various chores. He would not starve to death.

After breakfast he hiked to the edge of town and sat down beneath the shade of a big tree. He was tired of walking and decided there was nothing to be gained by doing so. He would wait until he was offered a ride. He had waited for almost an hour when he saw a cloud of dust coming down the road toward the opposite side of the small town. He watched with interest. Someone must be pushing his horses to raise so much dust. It was a hot day, and Stephen felt sorry for the poor animals, and then a moment later he realized that his sympathy was wasted. It was not a team and buggy that was approaching, but an automobile.

He got to his feet to see better. He had seen a number of cars in Chicago but only one since coming to Iowa. They were a rarity on Iowa's isolated country roads.

The automobile stopped near Stephen. Its driver got out, walked to the nearest house, and knocked on the door. Stephen watched while he went around to the back yard with the woman of the house. A few minutes later he returned to his automobile with a bucket of water. Interested and hopeful that he would be offered a ride, Stephen walked nearer.

It was the latest and fanciest car that Stephen had seen. Instead of the modified buggy wheels of most automobiles, this car had rubber-tired wheels about half the size of buggy wheels. It had a brass radiator, two acetylene head-lights, an acetylene light beside the seat, and what looked to be a top that could be raised and lowered. At present it was folded down along the rear of the back seat.

"Like it?" asked the man as he finished filling the radia-tor and replaced the ornamental cap.

"It's very nice," Stephen said politely. "Will it go very fast?"

"I've been moving right along at twenty miles an hour," the man said proudly. "That's the speed limit in this state, as you probably know."

Stephen didn't know but he nodded in agreement.

The man glanced at Stephen's bundle. "You look like you're going someplace," he observed.

"To Marshalltown," Stephen said. "Or rather to a little town not too far from there."

"I'm going pretty close to Marshalltown myself," the man said. "Would you care for a ride or are you afraid to ride in an automobile?"

"I'm not afraid," Stephen replied. "I'd like to try it."

"Hop in," the man ordered.

Stephen climbed in the car and put his bundle on the back seat. The driver adjusted the gas and spark, and got a heavy crank out from underneath the seat. He cranked four or five times; then the engine started with a roar. The car jounced and wiggled and shook, and Stephen was tempted to jump out. He held on to the side and waited bravely. The driver climbed in underneath the steering wheel, adjusted the cap on his head, covered his eyes with a pair of goggles, leaned over, and shouted, "We're off!" Reaching across Stephen, he released a hand brake which was on the right side of the car, he did something mysterious with another handle near the steering wheel, and the car started forward. It gained speed slowly, but in a few minutes was going down the road at a smart clip, leaving a huge billowing cloud of dust behind. The driver pointed to a speedometer and bellowed, "See that? We're going twenty-three miles an hour."

What wind there was, was from the east and fortunately they were able to leave the dust they created far behind. However, no matter how fast they went, they were unable to escape the odor of gasoline and hot grease. To Stephen it was very unpleasant, and he much preferred the smell of a horse.

"Did you ever go this fast before?" the man asked, shouting above the roar of his motor.

Stephen shook his head and then he remembered that he had ridden on a train. "On a train," he replied.

"Oh, well," the man said. "How about on a horse?"

Stephen was about to say no when he did some quick calculating. If Copper Lady ran a quarter of a mile in less than twenty-five seconds, that meant that she would take a hundred seconds to go a full mile. That would be more than thirty miles an hour.

"I've ridden a quarter horse," he bellowed back. "A quarter of a mile in less than twenty-five seconds."

The driver thought this over for several minutes. Obviously he was put out by the answer. Then he brightened. "Sure," he conceded. "But how long can he keep it up? This will keep going twenty miles an hour, hour after hour."

It was not an idle boast. For two hours they drove steadily at a speed of almost twenty miles an hour. Now and then they slowed up when they met a frightened team of work horses or when they passed through a small town. Shortly after twelve they stopped to eat. The driver parked in front of a café and in a minute there was an interested group of men around the car, some admiring and some critical.

"What is it?" one man asked. "Don't know as I've ever seen that make before."

"It's an EMF," the man replied. "It's manufactured by Studebaker now."

Obligingly he lifted the hood for their inspection.

"Four cylinders," he announced. "Develops thirty horse-power."

"It's a dang-fool contraption," one old-timer announced belligerently. "There ought to be a law keeping them off the road. All they do is scare the horses."

The owner of the car took up the challenge immedi-

ately. "Just wait, my friend," he predicted. "Some of
these days you're going to have to keep horses off the road
so they won't get in the way of automobiles. The horse
is on his way out."

The crowd roared with laughter at this ridiculous remark.

"If the horse is on his way out, so is man," one of the
onlookers remarked. "I don't know how you're going to
run a farm without a horse, but you can get by right
handy-like without an automobile. I'd like to see this
contraption of yours out there pulling a plow."

"Just wait; you will," the man announced confidently.

When they finished lunch, the salesman again cranked
the car and once more they started down the highway.
The car lived up to its owner's boast and ran steadily for
another three hours. Then the man turned north along an
intersecting highway.

"You're only about fourteen miles from Marshalltown, I
think. Now you've got to admit that you couldn't have
covered that much distance on a quarter horse."

Stephen agreed that he couldn't have. He thanked the
driver politely and watched while he disappeared down
the road behind a huge cloud of dust. Personally, he would
stick to horses.

For the next hour and a half he alternated between
walking along the dusty road in the hot afternoon sun
and resting beneath an occasional shade tree. No one was
going in his direction. For that matter, he was not too cer-

tain what direction he wanted to go. One passing farmer told him that the quickest way to reach Pitman was to avoid Marshalltown by going south and then east. However, no one else appeared to be going either south or east and as a result he made very little progress. He was tired, dusty, and sleepy. Discouraged, he sat down in the shelter of a solitary maple that was growing beside the road.

He couldn't even do a good job of running away, he thought bitterly. He had to limp along on his twisted foot while anyone else would be able to go twice as fast. He wished he had Copper Lady, but he didn't. As Hannah had made so clear, beggars did not have horses. And he was a beggar, a lame beggar sitting beside the road asking for a ride. The world was suddenly too much to face and he put his head down on his knees. He sat quietly and finally he dozed off.

He slept fitfully and was awakened about half an hour later by an odd clanking, rattling, ringing noise. He raised his head to see an enclosed wagon approaching drawn by a team of jet-black horses. Suspended on a wire above the back end of the wagon was an odd collection of pans, cans, and pots which jingled and rattled together as the wagon rolled along the road. As the wagon drew nearer, Stephen read the sign on its side. It said "Scissors and Knives Sharpened, Pots and Kettles Mended. Hiram Contest, Tinker."

Hiram Contest sat on the high front seat of his wagon singing to himself. He was a tall, lanky man with a long, thin nose, huge bushy eyebrows, and a black patch over one eye. He was headed in the right direction, so Stephen stepped forward hopefully. As he drew abreast, Hiram Contest stopped his jingling, noisy wagon and looked down at Stephen questioningly.

"Could I ride with you?" Stephen asked.

"I reckon you could if you can climb up here," Hiram Contest answered.

Stephen limped forward and climbed up, using the hub of the front wheel and the footrest which projected from the side of the high wagon. The driver glanced at Stephen's foot but said nothing. He took Stephen's bundle and placed it securely on the tall rack back of the seat. Then he gave a cluck to the team and they started forward again.

"You wouldn't be running away from home now, would you?" he asked.

"I don't really have a home," Stephen said, evading the question.

"Mothers and fathers are sort of peculiar people," Hiram Contest observed. "They sort of miss their kids and feel bad when they run away. Don't know why myself, since a lot of kids that I've seen run away aren't worth feeling bad about."

"My father and mother are dead," Stephen said quietly. "I've been living with an aunt and I know she'll be glad that I've gone."

"Then you are running away?"

Stephen thought about this for a minute. "No," he said

finally. "I'm going to join a good friend of mine. He runs a threshing outfit and he'll give me a job for the rest of the summer."

"Where is this threshing outfit?" Contest asked.

"Somewhere near a place called Pitman," Stephen replied. "I don't know exactly where."

"Well, I'm going to Burton, which is about seven or eight miles this side of Pitman," Contest replied. "This is Saturday night and there will be a lot of folks in town. Maybe some of them will know where your friend is."

Although Contest did not hurry his horses, they moved along briskly, and shortly after six o'clock they reached Burton. The sign at the city limits said "Burton, Iowa, population 683."

Burton was a small, sleepy town which reminded Stephen of Black Hawk. The dusty main street was deserted save for two figures seated on a familiar bench in front of the general store. One of these was wearing a blue uniform, a large star on his left breast, and a real six-shooter in a holster at his side. Hanging from the back of the bench was a short billy club attached to a leather thong. Hiram Contest pulled his team to a halt in front of the two men.

"Would it be all right if I parked my wagon someplace here on Main Street for two or three hours tonight?"

The town constable looked at him critically and apparently decided that Contest looked like an honest man. "Don't see no real reason why not," he replied. "Up there in front of the bank would be a good place."

Hiram Contest pulled his wagon over to the spot chosen and began unhitching his team. Stephen helped him and had his horse unhitched with the traces neatly looped up to the hames well before Contest was finished with his animal.

"You're a right handy man with a horse," Contest observed.

"I've worked in a livery stable," Stephen explained. "Would you like me to take the team someplace?"

"Don't know exactly where to take them," Contest replied. "I'd like to find somebody here in town that's got a small pasture. Suppose you stay with the wagon here while I ask out around."

Hiram Contest was gone approximately fifteen minutes and then he returned without his team.

"Found a fellow with a small pasture over that way about four blocks," he said. He glanced at the clock in the bank window. "We might as well go eat," he said. "The town won't begin to come to life for another fifteen or twenty minutes anyhow."

They found a café in the next block. After they had eaten, they returned to Contest's wagon. The side of the wagon nearest the sidewalk dropped down to form a large shelf or counter. Inside the wagon, Contest's grinding wheels, files, whetstone, blowtorch, soldering iron, and other tools were all placed ready for use. He checked his two acetylene lamps to make certain they would work when it grew darker. Then, after hanging up a number of placards stating that he had knives, scissors, teakettles, and pots for sale, he sat down to wait for the night's business.

Stephen climbed up to the driver's seat and from this point of vantage watched the town come slowly to life. Burton, like all Iowa towns at that time of the year, dozed during the long, hot, sunlit hours, its streets deserted, its stores empty, and its merchants waiting and preparing for Saturday night.

The first wagons arrived shortly after seven. The men and boys wore clean overalls and freshly laundered blue denim shirts while the girls wore cool ginghams and calicoes. The farm families were large and each wagon was filled with from four to fourteen children, ranging from small babies to young people who were practically full grown. The stores began to fill, the sidewalks became crowded, and Burton changed from a quiet, sleepy little town to a busy, noisy metropolis throbbing with life. Stephen had seen the same thing happen in Black Hawk, but Burton seemed especially lively and filled with people. There was a festive air about it. The children's faces had been scrubbed cleaner, the girls wore fancier dresses, and there was an air of excitement.

"Is something special going on tonight?" Hiram Contest asked an overalled loafer who stood leaning against his wagon.

"Yup," the man replied. "The band's going to parade tonight."

"What's the occasion?"

"They say that it's their tenth anniversary," the man replied. "That may be so, but the real reason is that they finally got money enough together to get themselves some new uniforms."

About eight-fifteen Stephen heard the distant tootling of horns as the band, somewhere out of sight, tuned up their instruments and prepared to march.

"Do you usually have this many people on a Saturday night or is there a special turnout because of the parade?" Contest asked.

"Burton does a right smart bit of business every Saturday night," the local resident replied. "However, there's a lot of people from over around Pitman tonight, just because of the band."

"It must be some band," Stephen observed.

"It is," the man said proudly. "You watch Jimmy True; he's the man with the trombone. He's quite a boy, Jimmy is."

"Good musician?" Hiram Contest asked.

"Well, I don't know that he's such a good musician. There's better in the band, but anyhow he's the star. Quite a boy."

There was a sudden end to the miscellaneous tootlings and a brief period of quiet as far as the band was concerned. Then there was a blare and the notes of "Yankee Doodle" floated out on the evening air. Stephen looked expectantly up the street and some minutes later he saw the band appear two blocks away. As it did, a hearty cheer went up from the crowd. The band deserved it. The band leader was twirling his baton in a fast-spinning arc, the men were stepping high, wide, and handsome. They were playing with all their might and at the same time were executing the complicated maneuver of rounding the corner. The new uniforms were resplendent. Neither Stephen nor anyone else in Burton had ever seen anything so fancy.

When the band was about a block distant, it finished its lively rendition of "Yankee Doodle" and struck into the "Stars and Stripes Forever" march. Hiram Contest appreciated music and he tapped his big foot in unison with it, rocking the whole wagon.

The band moved steadily onward and approached the spot where Contest had parked his wagon. Several doors away a farmer had unloaded his eggs and butter at the general store and his family had climbed out on the sidewalk to watch the parade. The farmer himself decided to wait and enjoy it, too.

"Now, you watch Jimmy True," their Burton gossiper advised with a chuckle.

Stephen had noticed the trombonist some distance down the street. He was a short, pudgy man with a round face that either was red from blowing his trombone or was naturally so. As the band came closer and closer, the man went through some rather peculiar gyrations. Although he had been marching on the left side of the band, he managed to cross over, working his way through the other players, until he was on the opposite side. One of his fellow members obligingly yielded his position, allowing the short trombonist to march on the edge of the band nearest the general store.

Although the trombonist was going through some rather violent motions, Stephen could hear no sound that he could definitely identify as coming from the trombone. He watched closely and decided that Jimmy True wasn't playing his trombone at all.

"He's not playing that trombone," he commented.

"Just wait, he will."

By this time the band was abreast of the farmer with his wagon and the horses were nervous and fidgety. The townspeople of Burton might think this was music but as far as the horses were concerned, it was hideous noise. The farmer watched the band with admiration but still kept an eye on his team and tightened his grip on the reins.

Jimmy True reached a position about four feet behind the horses. He closed his eyes, tilted his head back, pointed the trombone up toward the sky, and let go with the loudest, brassiest blare ever to come from a trombone. The team of horses acted as though doused by an ocean wave instead of a wave of sound. Their ears went back, their eyes rolled wildly, and their heads seemed to settle into their necks. They bunched their haunches like two scared rabbits, hesitated for a second, and then gave a mighty leap forward and went charging madly down the street. Jimmy True's trombone blared even louder; only this time it was a triumphant jeer. The crowd roared with laughter as the farmer sawed on his reins and the team plowed wildly down the street. Women yanked small children out of the way and everyone crowded back toward the sidewalks. The elderly man who had been talking to Hiram Contest and Stephen laughed until tears rolled down his cheeks. The team had long since disappeared before he got control of himself and wiped away the tears with a big red bandanna.

"I told you he was quite a boy," he chortled. "I've seen him cause as many as three runaways when he was really in top form on that trombone."

"Anybody get hurt?" Contest asked.

"No," the old man said derisively. "Not bad. A real good runaway is about as good clean fun as you can find, I always say. Most folks like them a lot better than a fight and nobody gets locked up in jail afterward."

"Somebody should," Hiram Contest observed dryly. "And I know just the man."

Stephen had not expected Hiram Contest to do much business on his street-corner stand, but he was mistaken. From the minute that the band passed out of view until ten o'clock Hiram was busy sharpening knives and scissors, mending pots and pans, or selling new ones.

About ten o'clock Stephen grew tired of his perch on the wagon seat and climbed down to make a tour of the business section. Burton was almost a replica of Black Hawk. The general store, the pool hall, the barbershop, and the cream and produce station were all familiar. As he walked down the street, Stephen paused now and then to ask if anyone knew the whereabouts of Simms, but no one could give him any information.

When he reached the livery stable, he felt a nostalgic twinge. He missed his Uncle Alf, he missed the horses, and he especially missed Copper Lady.

"Could you tell me if there's a man named Simms running a threshing rig anywhere around here?" he asked for the tenth time.

The four men in front of the stable fell silent at the question. They considered it soberly and then one asked, "What's he look like, son?"

"He's about your height," Stephen replied. "About forty or so. He's got a purple birthmark on the left side of his face."

"I know the man. He's that new fellow who took over the Bratton rig and is threshing for the Bledsoes and the Coolihans and that crowd." The speaker paused and looked at Stephen. "What do you want to find this Simms for?"

"He's a friend of mine and he'll give me a job," Stephen replied.

"Almost anybody will give you a job this time of the year," a second man observed. "Take my advice and stay away from those Bledsoes and Coolihans."

"Why?"

"They'll either work you to a shadow or else you'll get mixed up in one of their fights. They're working, fighting fools. There's Bledsoe twins and Coolihan twins, all of them boys about twenty or so. About two months ago the Bledsoe twins got engaged to the two Goodwin gals. That made the Coolihans pretty sore because they'd been courting the same gals. Those four boys have been scrapping all their lives and now with them all on the same threshing circuit, things will really pop. If everything doesn't blow up, including your friend's steam engine, I'll be surprised."

Chapter X

Threshing

THE FARMERS and their families began to leave Burton about ten-thirty and by eleven the little town was asleep again. Hiram Contest got his team, drove the wagon out to the edge of town, and parked it beneath a convenient tree. He loaned Stephen an extra blanket and the two of them slept on the ground underneath the wagon. They awoke shortly after dawn the next morning to a clear, sunlit day.

"I'm headed in the direction you want to go," Contest told Stephen, "and I don't think I've worked this section of the country before, so I'll be visiting each farmhouse. If you want to stay with me, we'll locate that friend of yours sooner or later. But today is Sunday and Sunday is my day off. I stay put wherever I am."

Monday morning they drove out of town about five miles to be out of the probable area of those who patronized Contest Saturday night. Then the scissors man began calling on each farm in turn. During the morning and early part of the afternoon Contest found plenty of work sharpening scissors and mending pans, but after three-thirty they found no one home at most of the farmhouses.

"This may not be your friend's circuit but someone's threshing around here," Contest observed. "There's no womenfolk at home, and if you've noticed, most of the teams and wagons are gone."

Half a mile down the road they located a threshing rig. The countryside had been dotted with shocks of golden grain, but on this farm the fields had been stripped and only the flat land with its yellow stubble remained. In the distance, above a grove of trees, they could see a column of black smoke wafting lazily up into the hot afternoon sky while nearby there was a cloud of dust.

"Chaff," Contest said in answer to Steve's question. "When the threshing machine blows out the straw there's always a lot of chaff that floats up into the air."

"There's two wagons," Stephen said, pointing to the far corner of the field.

The two wagons were fitted with hayracks and both had been loaded with enormous loads of wheat sheaves. A man was on top of each one while two other men stood on the ground pitching up the last few remaining bundles.

"They look like the day was just starting instead of finishing," Contest observed. "Look at those fellows go."

The big teams moved along at a lively clip while the men on the ground were pitching furiously to keep up with them. They came to the last shock of grain, which

the two loaders divided between them. When the last
bundles came sailing through the air, the drivers did not
pause but turned their horses almost in unison and headed
toward the clump of trees that hid the farmhouse. The
men on the ground had to race to catch up. One man threw
his pitchfork high in the air and it landed miraculously on
the top of the load. He leaped, caught hold of the rack,
and climbed nimbly up the back. The other raced for his
wagon with pitchfork still in hand, finally catching it only
after it had gone several hundred yards.

"Look at them push those horses," Contest observed.
"Those boys are in a powerful hurry."

They reached the lane leading to the farm and lost
sight of the distant wagons. As they drove down the lane
they could hear a distant clatter and whirring and the
unmistakable puffing of a steam engine. Then they entered
the farmyard, rounded the corncrib, and looked into the
lot behind the red barn. There, surrounded by a tangle of
horses and wagons, was a big threshing machine. From the
end of its long spout straw poured forth in a steady stream,
adding layer after layer to a towering semicircular golden
stack. Some distance away, connected by an enormously
long, flat leather belt, sat the steam engine, radiating heat
and noise and spewing forth clouds of black smoke. Seated
at the throttle was a grimy soot-blackened man with a huge
smile on his face. The soot did not mislead Stephen, but
the smile did. He had to look twice before he was certain
that he had found Simms.

"There he is," he told Hiram Contest happily.

"I'm glad you found him," Contest replied. "Go on over and make yourself known. I'll go up to the house and talk to the womenfolk. I'd rather talk to a pretty woman any time than to a thresher all covered with dust and soot."

Stephen started to thank his scissor-grinding friend but Contest shooed him on his way. "We'd better say good-by now," Contest said. "I doubt if I'll stay for long."

Since Simms was not expecting Stephen and certainly not as a passenger on a tinker's wagon, he paid no attention as Stephen approached. Stephen walked within a few feet of the big steam engine and gazed at it in admiration. It was an enormous machine with huge iron-lugged wheels and above them a big belt wheel over which the flat leather belt rotated. The other end of the long belt was connected to the thresher or separator some sixty feet away. The engine hissed and clanked and puffed and vibrated. Simms was up on the engine platform and above him was a flat sheet-metal canopy which stretched from one end of the engine to the other. It and the other metal parts of the engine had been painted a dark green with bright red trim. A number of the fittings, however, were brass and these had been brightly polished. In spite of the black smoke which poured from the stack and the grease which is part of the lifeblood of any engine, Simms's machine was as neat and as clean as it is possible for a steam engine to be. As Stephen stood watching, Simms reached forward, inspected something carefully, and then with loving care wiped a spot of grease from the shiny paintwork.

Simms had changed. The lanky man with the purple birthmark was no longer the quiet, retiring man of Frisbee's livery stable. Instead, he was a calm and confident engineer. There was an assurance about every movement that he made. He was an expert. The labors of these two dozen brawny farmers and the work of all those fat-rumped work horses meant nothing without Simms's equipment and knowledge. While threshing season lasted, he was king. The harvest of dozens of farmers depended on him.

"Hi, Bob, it's me—Stephen!" Steve said, moving around to where Simms could see him.

Simms looked doubtfully at the waving boy in front of him and then recognition dawned. He gave a happy wave and jumped down from his shaky, noisy engine.

"Steve!" he shouted above the hiss of the steam. "What in the world are you doing here?"

"I came to find you," Steve replied. "I want a job."

Simms raised both eyebrows and looked at Stephen intently. "Leave home?" he asked.

Stephen nodded. "I'll tell you about it later."

"We're just about finished here," Simms said. He nodded toward two towering loads of bundles that had rounded the corner of the grove. "Here come the last two loads now, I think." He stood beside Steve for a moment watching, and then said, "Come up on the engine with me. That looks like the Coolihan and the Bledsoe boys and if so, I've got to put on more steam."

The two wagons coming in from the field pulled up behind the two that were feeding the separator and waited impatiently for their turn. Stephen had followed Simms up onto the steel floor plates of the steam engine and he was absorbed with all the valves, gauges, and other mysterious parts. Simms reached over and tapped him on the shoulder.

"Watch these boys," he advised, a grin on his face. "If they don't wreck my machinery by feeding it too fast, they'll shorten this threshing run by a good five days. Never saw such madmen in my life."

The two wagons which had been feeding the separator tossed their last few bundles of oats onto the feeder platform and moved away simultaneously. Their places were taken immediately by the two wagons which had just arrived. Stephen had no idea which were the Bledsoe twins and which were the Coolihans, but it made little difference. As far as appearances were concerned, the four men might have been quadruplets. All four were young men in their early twenties. They were of medium height but their barrel-like torsos made them look short. Stephen had seen pictures of gorillas, and these four reminded him for all the world of those huge, shaggy beasts. They had enormous broad shoulders and long, swinging arms, powerful legs, and short, powerful necks. Their faces were somewhat more attractive than a gorilla's, but they looked almost as wild and unpredictable.

As soon as the two wagons were in position, the four men picked up their pitchforks and began tossing their bundles furiously onto the feeder platform. In less than a minute they had practically deluged the tall man who fed the bundles from the platform into the separator.

"Take it easy, you blithering idiots!" he bellowed.

"Let me feed it," one of the four men shouted in return.

"Come ahead."

One of the young men from the wagon on the right made a wild leap and managed to land on the feeder platform. He teetered precariously for a minute, and then found his balance. He took the fork from the tall man's hand and began furiously feeding bundles into the machine.

Simms shook his head. "This circuit's going to take ten years off my life," he said, but he was grinning. "That lunatic might have fallen into the thresher. I never could have stopped this machine. He'd have come out through that spout in little pieces."

"Which one is he?" Stephen asked.

"One of the Bledsoes," Simms replied. "One's called Tiny and the other one Big Boy. Don't ask me why, 'cause they're both the same size."

The Bledsoe twin on the thresher platform turned toward the steam engine and roared in a voice that could be heard for a quarter of a mile, "Give her more steam! What are we waiting for?"

Simms reached up, pulled the throttle, and the clanking and hissing of the engine took on a new tempo. The whine and roar of the separator increased and straw spewed out even faster from the long spout.

The Bledsoe on the separator worked furiously and managed to clear it of oat bundles. Then he turned to the Coolihans and roared at them triumphantly, "What's the matter? You wearing out?" he asked. "Feed me some bundles."

The Coolihans bellowed some insult in return and went to work in earnest. They tossed the oat bundles up so fast that a steady stream of them descended upon the platform. In a minute they were piled high around him and some were tumbling off on the other side of the machine. Bledsoe refused to cry quits, however. He tossed his fork aside in disgust and began throwing the bundles into the separator with his bare hands. Simms opened the throttle even wider and the machinery took on a high-pitched whine.

"I hope it will hold together for another five minutes," he bellowed at Stephen. However, he did not appear worried. The Bledsoe twin on the wagon stopped feeding bundles in order to give his brother a chance, and in a few minutes the Coolihan wagon was empty. Slowly the twin on the feeder platform dug out from under and fed the last of the bundles into the threshing machine. Then his brother unloaded the remainder of his wagon. By this time the two Coolihans had driven their empty wagon around the engine. They stopped a few feet away from the Bledsoe wagon and watched the last of the unloading, making taunting remarks which Stephen could not hear because of the distance. Whatever they said must have been annoying, for when the Bledsoe boy reached the last bundle on his wagon, instead of throwing it up on the threshing machine feeder platform, he turned and hurled it at the two Coolihans.

One of the Coolihan twins reached up and deftly caught the bundle, shouting something at the Bledsoe twin who pitched it. Just then the Bledsoe boy on the feeder platform bellowed, "All clear, last bundle in," in a voice that could be heard for miles. Simms waited several minutes until the last of the chaff had been blown from the long spout and grain no longer trickled from the grain spout.

Then he closed the throttle, pulled back a lever, and sudden silence descended over the farm. Strange sounds that had been drowned in the roar of the engine and the drone of the separator suddenly came to life. Men's voices seemed oddly loud and clear, and Stephen could hear the restless stirring of tired horses, anxious to go home. All that remained of the threshing noise was the steady hiss of steam. Simms reached up and pulled a cord twice, and two shrill blasts from the steam whistle split the air. The threshing day was done.

"Well, boys, that was a right smart day's work," a tall, elderly man in overalls said. He pulled out a big gold watch from the bib of his overalls and consulted it.

"We're finished in good time, too," he announced. "I think that's the shortest time we ever threshed this farm."

"We'd have been through at least an hour earlier if we'd had two good workers instead of those two Bledsoe boys with their lace drawers," one of the Coolihans remarked.

"Get down off that wagon and I'll show you who's got lace drawers," one of the Bledsoes answered.

Both of the Coolihans climbed down from their wagon. The Bledsoe boy who'd issued the challenge handed the reins to his brother and said, "Here, Big Boy, take these," and leaped over the edge of the hayrack.

The three men met midway between the two wagons. Tiny Bledsoe and the one Coolihan twin eyed each other warily while the remaining Coolihan with no one to face him looked up at Big Boy Bledsoe and said, "Looks like you're scared to get down."

"Why don't you come up and get me?" Big Boy Bledsoe replied.

The Coolihan twin did not need to be invited twice. He started toward the wagon.

"If there's going to be a fight, it's going to be fair and square," the tall man with the watch declared. "Besides, you got to be in shape for threshing over at Grant's tomorrow morning come six."

"Give them two rounds of three minutes each," somebody suggested. "Simms, you blow the whistle."

"Good idea," said the tall, elderly man who apparently was the owner of the farm. He held up his hand. "All right, let her go."

Simms blew an ear-splitting blast on the whistle.

Everyone's attention was centered on Tiny Bledsoe and the Coolihan twin who were on the ground. In the meantime the other Coolihan boy had climbed over the edge of the hayrack, stepping into the Bledsoe wagon. Big Boy Bledsoe did not wait for any whistle. As soon as Coolihan stepped over the edge of the rack and both hands were free, Big Boy Bledsoe swung with a haymaker that landed squarely on Coolihan's jaw. Coolihan staggered backward, half-falling against the rack. As he did so, he let out a bellow that was a mixture of pain and anger. At this instant Simms blew his starting whistle.

The Bledsoes were driving a huge team of grays. While

the big horses were tired after a hard day's work, they were also nervous and upset by the crowd that had gathered so near. The sound of the steam whistle and the roar of pain from Coolihan upset them. They started forward, not running away, but apparently anxious to get away from the crowd with all its noise and confusion. They pulled away from the separator, circled in front of the Coolihan wagon, and at a fast trot headed toward the lane leading out to the road. Neither Big Boy Bledsoe nor the Coolihan twin with him in the wagon paid any attention whatsoever to the horses. Instead, they were standing in the middle of the wagon swinging wildly at each other, now and then connecting. Stephen watched in amazement as the horses disappeared down the lane.

A few of the threshers looked up, but when they saw that the team was not actually running away they paid no further attention. Meanwhile, Tiny Bledsoe and the other Coolihan twin were engaged in a hot-and-heavy slugging match on the ground. Both were wild fighters, swinging hard and wide and depending on luck rather than science. Now and then one of them would land a good solid punch and a cheer would go up from those watching. The onlookers were completely impartial. They would cheer a good solid punch no matter who made it.

"Two minutes," Simms announced, consulting his watch. "One minute to go in this round."

Before the minute had scarcely begun, however, there was a sudden onslaught from another quarter. About eight women armed with brooms, sticks, mops, and carpet beaters swept into view, rolling onward like a tidal wave. They brushed the watching men out of the way as though they were flies and then fell savagely on the two fighters. They made no distinction whatsoever but beat both men around their heads and shoulders with their mops and brooms and sticks. In a second it was all over. Simms blew his whistle about five times and the tall man with the watch shouted, "Fight's over. The winner—the sunbonnet brigade."

The men roared with laughter. A tall woman in a sunbonnet and faded gray dress stood with one hand on her hip and another on a broom handle. "There'll be no fighting on this farm," she announced. "And we women have just taken a vote. There'll be no fighting during threshing season if we can prevent it. If there's any fighting before noon, there'll be no dinner, and don't think we don't mean it."

The men grinned and winked at each other, but they said nothing.

"I guess even the Coolihans and the Bledsoes will behave during the morning," Simms observed. "Although I'm not sure they wouldn't rather fight than eat."

The men rapidly dispersed and soon the big farmyard was empty save for two teams belonging to Mr. Blodgett, the big tank wagon that Simms used to haul water, and the threshing rig.

"You're going to stay for supper, aren't you?" the tall

man with the watch asked Simms.

"Thanks a lot, but I think I'll move on over to Grant's farm," Simms replied. "I've got steam up now and it's still early enough so that I can get there in time for supper."

He climbed down from his engine with Stephen following. Together they took off the big belt and rolled it up. As they readied the rig for moving to the next farm, Stephen told Simms what had happened back in Black Hawk.

"Well, you're certainly welcome to stay with me as long as you want," Simms said heartily. "I'm tickled to death that you're here, 'cause I certainly need a man. I had an old fellow all lined up, but at the last minute he changed his mind and went down to Missouri to visit his son."

In half an hour they were ready to roll. They hooked the threshing machine behind the steam engine and behind it the water wagon, and then, with the steam engine snorting and puffing, they started slowly down the lane. The big pointed lugs on the wide tractor wheels kicked up clouds of dirt as they went along and left the surface of the lane looking oddly pockmarked.

"Looks like a good engine," Stephen said as they slowly rolled toward the road.

"It's a good rig," Simms replied. "It needed a few repairs. The man that owned it hadn't done much about spit and polish, but he kept her in pretty good mechanical shape. Twenty-five hundred dollars for the whole shebang. Why, it's worth at least twice that! I'll have it paid for in no time." He patted the throttle affectionately. "I've named her Helen," he announced.

"Why?" Stephen asked.

" 'Cause the prettiest girl I ever knew was named Helen," Simms replied. "Also she was the hottest-tempered woman I ever knew, always blowing off steam about something."

During the next few days Stephen learned a great deal about the life of a thresher. It was interesting and exciting but it was not easy. Usually he and Simms pulled into the yard of the next farm to be threshed late at night. They would set the separator or threshing machine in position, place the steam engine, chock its wheels, unroll the big flat belt, and heave and tug until it was in place on the driving wheel. Then they would bank the fire of the engine, wash the grime and dirt from their hands and faces, and wearily turn in for a short night's sleep. Although occasionally there were extra beds, most of the time they slept in the hayloft, often too weary to bother removing their clothes.

The day began early. At four o'clock they rolled out to stoke the boiler fire. Stephen's job was to make certain that the water wagon was well filled.

The first wagons from nearby farms arrived shortly after six. The farmers, too, had been up since four o'clock. They had milked the cows, fed the hogs, eaten breakfast, harnessed up the horses, then perhaps driven three or four miles. When they arrived, they went immediately into the fields. The wheat or oats, which had been cut several weeks before and bound into sheaves or bundles, was waiting in row after row of golden shocks. As the first wagonload of bundles rolled into the farmyard the owner would breathe a sigh of relief. Once more he had beaten the weather to the harvest. By this time Simms had finished his greasing and oiling of the separator and engine. When he received a signal that a grain wagon was under the grain spout and the long blower pipe was pointed toward the site where the farmer wanted his straw stack, he gave one long toot on the whistle, which meant that the steam pressure was up and that Helen was ready to thresh wheat. From the moment the first bundle entered the machine, the men worked furiously to keep its cavernous maw supplied. Wagon after wagon jolted in from the fields and as one man tired on the feeder platform he was replaced by another. Six to eight men pitched bundles in the field, there were usually seven or eight men on the bundle wagons, three or four more with grain wagons were needed to haul the grain away, and usually one or two men were required to build the straw stack properly. As the day wore on and the sun climbed in the sky, rivulets of perspiration ran down the men's backs, across their faces, and salty water dripped from their eyebrows into their eyes. Smoke billowed forth from Helen's stack and those on the windward side of her choked and sputtered in the fumes, smoke, and soot. Surrounding everything was chaff; the straw spewed forth from the long blowpipe and while the large pieces landed on the stack the small bits swirled and circled through the air for yards around. Everyone's nose and mouth were filled with small bits of straw. It settled in their hair, their eyes, their ears, their pockets, and their shoes. With the heat and the chaff there was never-ending noise. The big belt flapped and slapped, the engine hissed and clanked, and the separator droned on and on with a high-pitched whine. The shouting of the men to their teams and to each other was lost in the over-all din.

By noontime every man was soaked with perspiration and had drunk at least a gallon of water. There was never any need to ring the dinner bell. The women of the household would simply inform Simms and he would blow the whistle once and stop the steam engine. The sudden and welcome quiet attracted more attention than any noise possibly could have done.

Dinner was the high point of the day. It made all the work, the sweat, and the lack of sleep worth-while.

Some of the men washed at the stock watering trough while others used the basins which were placed on the back porch. The dozens of roller towels and the snow-white feed sacks were usually dingy and dirty within a few minutes from men rubbing off dirt rather than washing it off. They soaked their hair, ran a comb through it, and then sat down at one of the benches beside the big plank tables under the trees. The dinners left Stephen agape. Each woman tried to outdo the one before her on the circuit. She and her daughters and perhaps several relatives from town were busy for days ahead baking and cooking. There were heaping platters of fried chicken, roast loins of pork, whole hams, mountains of mashed potatoes, and huge wash pitchers full of brown gravy. There were string beans and peas and carrots and corn and beets and turnips. There were boiled cabbage, coleslaw, noodles, and hot biscuits. There were always at least five kinds of jelly and preserves. Each woman that helped brought her special pickles. The big tables groaned under the weight of food, but as the hungry threshers sat down before it, it began to magically disappear. Most of them ate a portion of everything and came back for seconds, and then, finally, there was the climax—the dessert. A washboiler of coffee was brought out, three or four huge buckets of milk, and the pie. There were strawberry pie, blackberry pie, apple, peach, and raisin. Stephen's favorite was gooseberry. After the pie one could choose from four or five different kinds of cake, but somehow Stephen never seemed able to get as far as the cake. He could never remember all that was coming and he invariably ran out of space.

After dinner the men relaxed in the shade for a few minutes. They told stories, joked, and poked fun at each other, while the Coolihans and the Bledsoes argued and threatened to start another fight.

The period of rest was short, however, and soon the noise and confusion began again, and once more the wagons rolled in from the fields and the straw stack grew higher and higher and higher. Some farmers built frames ahead of time and blew straw on top of them, making a warm straw house for their cattle with walls of straw ten or fifteen feet thick.

Stephen hauled water, stoked the boiler fires, and when Simms had adjustments to make on the separator, he sat at the throttle. He soon learned how to operate the big steam engine and in a few days had earned the nickname of Little Chief Engineer. This was shortened to Little Chief, and when the men saw that he was a willing and able worker he was accepted as part of the gang.

Although the farmers were brawny, hardfisted, hard-muscled workers, the Bledsoes and the Coolihans were the drivers. They set the pace. Everything was a contest as far as they were concerned. They competed to see who could haul the most loads of bundles, who could stack the loads the highest, and who could pitch them to the thresh-ing machine platform the fastest. While they worked and raced they taunted each other with being lazy, slow, and inept. Although both pairs seemed able to engage in good-natured joking with anyone else, their jibes and remarks to each other always held the hint of ill-temper and anger.

The two Goodwin girls, to whom the Bledsoes were engaged, were the daughters of one of the farmers on the threshing circuit. Since each farm wife usually had eight or ten other neighboring women to help her when she served the threshing dinner, the Goodwin girls were often present. When they were, the rivalry between the Bledsoes and the

Coolihans grew worse, if possible.

"It's tough enough trying to keep up with those crazy Coolihans and Bledsoes," remarked one older farmer, "but when those two Goodwin gals are here those boys go berserk. The Bledsoe boys are trying to show off and the Coolihans are trying to show them up. I don't know which are worse."

Twice during Stephen's first week with the threshing crew fights between the sets of twins were stopped. Once one of the Coolihans ran the Bledsoe wagon into the ditch, breaking a wheel. This had happened in the field and there were several minutes of battle before anyone realized what was taking place. As a result one of the Coolihans had a black eye and one of the Bledsoes a raw cheekbone the rest of the week.

The long work-filled days went by with incredible speed and suddenly, when it seemed the week had scarcely begun, it would be Sunday again. Simms would spend most of that day repairing minor damage to his machinery and making various adjustments which he felt were necessary. He fussed over his huge steam engine like a hen over a tiny chick. His work produced results, however, for the engine ran perfectly and no time was lost through breakdowns. The rivalry between the Bledsoes and the Coolihans also speeded up the work. The weeks followed one another until suddenly Stephen realized that he had been gone from home one month. The fields for several miles around, which had been dotted with golden shocks, were now empty. The weather had been as nearly perfect as possible for bringing in the harvest. It had rained on four successive Sundays, which gave the other crops the water they needed but did not slow the threshing.

The last three farms to be threshed belonged to the Coolihans, the Bledsoes, and the Goodwins, and when the rig arrived at the first of these, there was a truce called in the running battle between the twins. The Coolihans felt it would be inhospitable to attack the Bledsoes while they were guests on their farm and the Bledsoes returned the favor. The Goodwin farm was considered neutral territory because the quarrelsome four felt that brawling would show lack of respect to the two Goodwin girls. A strange peace and quiet descended over the threshing operations for the last few days of the run. Oddly enough, the continual competition, the constant jibes, taunting, and insults were missed by the rest of the crew. When the workers assembled on the last day, which was the second day at the Goodwin farm, and the two Bledsoe boys did not appear, there was genuine disappointment.

"I figured we'd wind up this season with a real bang-up, drag-out fight," one brawny farmer remarked. "It's been building up for a month now. It's a shame to get up such a big head of steam and not blow the safety valve."

"Maybe the Goodwin gals figured that would happen and they made the Bledsoe boys stay away," one of the men suggested.

The Bledsoe twins had hired two men to take their

places, but the substitutes made no explanation as to why
the Bledsoe boys had not appeared themselves. All hands
agreed that no ordinary cause could have kept them away.
The last day of threshing was almost a celebration. A mid-
day meal to end all meals was served, and the entire day
was as much a party as a day of work.

All hands pitched in with a will and by noon there were
scarcely two hours of work remaining. The crew paused
for an extra-long noon hour. In all the bustle and confusion
and high spirits it was not until the meal was half over that
someone remarked that neither of the Goodwin girls was
helping serve the long tables.

"Where's Sally and Marge?" one of the Coolihan twins
asked Mrs. Blodgett as she put several pies on the table.

"In the kitchen, I guess," she replied in an offhand way.

"They weren't in the kitchen when I went in to help
carry out that big pot of coffee," a redheaded young man
observed.

"Mighty peculiar," one man remarked. "The Bledsoe
twins both gone and now Sally and Marge not around.
Looks mighty suspicious to me."

In a few minutes the news was out. The two Bledsoe
boys and the Goodwin girls had slipped off quietly to be
married. There was great shouting and cheering and talk up
and down the table. Everyone seemed happy except the
two Coolihans, who tried to take the news good-naturedly.
Everyone also considered the secret wedding a challenge.
The two young couples, by not having a large wedding

and inviting everyone to a wedding dinner, had played an outrageous trick on the threshing circuit. Something had to be done in retaliation.

For the next two hours there was speculation and discussion as the crews brought in the last of the oats. As the last load of bundles drew up to the machine, there was a new and optimistic note. Everyone's spirits brightened. From some mysterious source, there had apparently been good news.

When the last grain had trickled down the grain chute and no more straw came from the long pipe, Simms closed Helen's throttle and gave five triumphant toots on her whistle. The threshing season had ended. The crew gathered around and gave a lusty cheer and then trouped once more to the big tables, this time for ice cream and lemonade to celebrate the conclusion of a job well done. They congratulated Simms on his smoothly operating rig, Stephen on his job as assistant chief engineer, and each other on a bountiful harvest. Then as every man was finishing his second plate of ice cream the word went from one to another around the big table. "Shivaree tonight. Meet at nine o'clock at Danny Breese's."

Chapter XI

The Shivaree

ALTHOUGH the job was finished on the threshing circuit, Simms had agreed to thresh some grain for several farmers who belonged to no organized group. These men had small amounts of grain and had stacked their bundles and covered the stacks with tarpaulins. There was little to fear from the weather and Simms decided to wait a day before moving.

"The Goodwins have invited us to stay here several days if we want," he told Stephen. "I'd like to do a few little repair jobs on the engine and I think we both could stand a little time off. This stacked grain will take another week and then we can start looking for a sawmill job for the winter."

Shortly before dark, Dan Monroe, a young man who had been one of the threshers, stopped by in his buggy. He was a cousin of the Goodwin girls and he claimed to be paying a friendly visit. Mr. and Mrs. Goodwin, however, were secretive and suspicious.

"He's trying to find out where the Bledsoe boys and their brides went after the wedding," Simms told Stephen as they walked outside. "I heard some of the men saying that they figured they were going to Omaha on their honeymoon. However, I doubt if they went too far today."

A few minutes later Dan Monroe came out and untied his horse.

"Aren't you two coming along?" he asked. "I've got plenty of room."

"Not me," said Simms. "I want to get some sleep, but if Stephen here wants to go, there's no reason why he can't sleep tomorrow."

"Come on, Little Chief," Dan urged. "If you haven't been to a shivaree, you're just plain ignorant."

"Let me change my shirt," Stephen replied, "and I'll be with you."

When they arrived at Danny Breese's, there were at least twenty buggies, a half-dozen riding horses, and a number of young people on foot. Altogether there were probably fifty or sixty present. Danny Breese had taken unofficial charge of operations. He climbed up on the back of one of the buggies and addressed the group.

"It's a right smart turnout we've got here tonight, folks," he said with a broad grin, "and I imagine you're all set to make some noise."

Everyone responded by screaming, whistling, yelling, and ringing bells. There were sleigh bells, dinner bells, sheep bells, and cow bells. Others beat on pots and pans and washtubs.

Breese held up a hand for silence.

"I can see you all came prepared," he announced. "Well, let's save the noise until later. Now, first off, I want to warn everybody that we don't know anything for certain. We have a tip that the two honeymooning couples are holed up near Jefferson at a farm belonging to an aunt of the Goodwin gals. Most of you folks know the aunt. It's Mrs. Henry Gault, who used to live near here. Dan Monroe was over to the Goodwins' tonight and tried to get a little bit of information but they weren't talking. We aren't positive about things, but the way we figure it is this: The best driving team at the Bledsoes' is still there, and Goodwin still has all his horses, so the honeymooners couldn't have planned to go far by buggy. One of the gals let drop that they hoped to spend a few days honeymooning in Omaha. That means traveling by train. They didn't get married until eleven o'clock this morning, too late to catch the one train going west that stops near here, so we figure they're spending the night at this aunt's, and will catch the train at Jefferson in the morning. As I said before, we might be wrong. It's about a twelve-mile ride and you may ride over there and back, all for nothing. If you are still willing to go under those conditions, let's get going."

The prospect of a twelve-mile ride in the moonlight sounded attractive to most of those gathered in the Breese farmyard whether or not there was a shivaree at the end of it. In a few minutes a long procession of buggies and wagons streamed out of the farmyard and headed westward.

Stephen rode with Dan Monroe, another young man, and two young women.

The night was unusually cool for mid-August and very comfortable for riding. The horses jogged along briskly under a brilliant full moon and soon everyone was singing. Several people had brought mandolins and banjos and the procession moved tunefully and happily through the beautiful Iowa night.

"They call this a 'belling' back where I used to live in Pennsylvania," one of the girls remarked between songs.

"Whatever you call them, they're a lot of fun," Dan Monroe observed from his front seat in the buggy.

"Sometimes I think they're kind of mean," one of the girls observed. "They get out of hand."

"One certainly got out of hand over at Bill Dorflinger's two years ago," the other young man in the buggy said with a chuckle. "We serenaded there for about an hour and young Dorflinger and his bride wouldn't come out, so finally someone found a ladder and climbed up on top of the roof and stuck some gunny sacks in the chimney. It was fall, and they had a fire going in the kitchen and we thought we'd smoke them out. Instead, we came close to burning the house down."

"I'm afraid of what those crazy Coolihans will do tonight," said the girl who had lived in Pennsylvania. "They don't like the Bledsoe twins, and what's more I don't think they have much common sense."

About half a mile from their destination the procession

stopped and two of the men went ahead on foot as scouts. After about fifteen minutes they returned with the news that the house was dark and apparently everyone had gone to sleep.

"There's a big grove of trees between the house and the road," Danny Breese announced happily. "We can drive up close and tie the horses to the fence. Then we'll go into the farmyard on foot. Everybody keep as quiet as they can until I shoot off the shotgun."

Twenty minutes later, to the accompaniment of giggles, low-voiced warnings, and many sh-h-hs from the leader, everyone filed into the farmyard and grouped themselves around the house. If anyone was awake inside, he gave no sign. Suddenly the roar of a shotgun split the quiet night. Instant bedlam followed. Bells clanged and pealed, pans and kettles banged and rattled, someone blew mightily on a brass horn, and someone thumped on an old water barrel. After several minutes of racket, someone in the house lighted a kerosene lamp in one of the second-floor rooms. A moment later a pair of white shoulders projected through an upstairs window.

"What do you want?" a pleasant voice asked. "What are you making all that noise for?"

"We want the Bledsoe boys and their brides," Danny Breese called out.

"Bledsoe boys? Are they married?" the woman asked in a surprised voice.

There was a roar from the crowd. When it had quieted,

Instant bedlam followed.

Danny Breese replied, "You can't fool us, Mrs. Gault. We know they're here. We looked in the barn and found an extra buggy."

Mrs. Gault said nothing but withdrew her shoulders from the window and pulled down the blind. The clanging and banging broke out with renewed fury. This time there were shouts of "Come on down or we'll come up and get you." Several more minutes passed, and then lights appeared in several second-story windows. Finally one of the Bledsoe boys stuck his head out a window.

"All right," he called good-naturedly. "We'll be down. Just give us a little time to get dressed."

The crowd showed their approval by banging and clanging and cheering even louder.

While the occupants of the house dressed, the serenaders brought their horses, with their buggies and wagons, into the farmyard and tethered them wherever they could find room. Lights went on in the kitchen, and a few minutes later Mrs. Gault appeared at the back door, her long hair hastily pinned up in an untidy pile above her round, good-natured face.

"We didn't think you'd locate them here, but I baked some pies and cakes just in case. You've had a long drive, so you deserve to sit down and have something to eat. Come on in."

The noisy group filed into the big farm kitchen and its adjoining dining room. The two Goodwin girls appeared, looking rather embarrassed, but with good-natured smiles on their faces. Behind them were their husbands, the Bledsoe twins. As the four entered the kitchen the house shook with the racket of bells, whistles, and banging pans. When it finally subsided, Mrs. Gault held up her hand.

"Now I'm going to put a stack of plates here, some pies, some cake, some whipped cream, some milk, and some coffee. You'll have to help yourselves."

The two brides attempted to help Mrs. Gault, but she brushed them away. "You can't work on your wedding night," she insisted. "My cousin's visiting me and she'll be down in a minute. That's all the help I need."

Stephen was standing near the kitchen door waiting quietly until the crowd moved away from the table. He had caught a glimpse of the huge blackberry and peach pies when Mrs. Gault brought them in from the pantry. They looked delicious. He started to move toward the table when something caused him to look toward the stairs. Standing in the doorway was the familiar figure of Hannah Frisbee. Her face wore her usual cold, disapproving look and her lips were pressed together in a straight line.

"Folks, I want you to meet my cousin Hannah Frisbee," Mrs. Gault announced in a hearty voice which carried above the noisy crowd. "She's from Black Hawk, Iowa, and is visiting here for a few days."

Hannah forced a faint smile and nodded around the room. It was obvious that she did not approve of shivarees.

With apprehension that was close to panic Stephen

edged toward the back door. Hannah moved toward the kitchen table to help her cousin serve the pie and cake. For a moment Stephen was certain that she would see him; and then the broad shoulders of Tom Blodgett came between them as a screen. Hastily, Stephen opened the screen door to the kitchen and slipped outside. Quietly he limped through the darkness until he was in the shadow of the big lilac bush by the yard gate. He sat down there to wait. He was hungry and that pie was tempting, but he would rather starve than risk being seen by Hannah Frisbee.

He had been sitting beneath the bush about five minutes when three shadowy figures came toward him from the barnyard. They paused by the gate and Stephen recognized the Coolihan twins and another young man who was often with them, Don Henshaw.

"All right, now," said one of the Coolihan boys. "You go in and when you get a chance to talk to either one of the Bledsoes on the q.t., tell him somebody's trying to fix his buggy so it'll break down in the morning. Wait about ten minutes and if he doesn't come back, then tell the other one the same thing."

"Right," Don replied.

He went inside and the two Coolihan boys disappeared in the shadowy farmyard. Several minutes passed and then Tiny Bledsoe came hurrying down the path toward the gate. For a moment Stephen considered warning him, but decided to follow instead. He tried to keep Tiny in sight by slipping from shadow to shadow, but he soon lost the hurrying young groom. A moment later he heard the sound of scuffling and a muffled shout. He reached the corncrib and peered cautiously around the corner. Tiny Bledsoe was flat on his back in the dusty farmyard and the two Coolihan boys were on top of him, busily tying his hands and legs. His mouth had been stuffed with a rag and the gag tied securely in place.

Stephen watched while they finished tying the prone figure. Then one of the Coolihans picked up the victim as though he weighed nothing and tossed him over his shoulder. He carted him over to their spring wagon and threw him unceremoniously on the bed of straw.

"Well, that's one of them," one of the Coolihans remarked. "Let's go back and wait for Big Boy."

The point of ambush was apparently beside the corncrib, for they hurried back in that direction.

Stephen waited until they had disappeared and then peered over the edge of the wagon. Tiny Bledsoe was writhing and turning violently but he was completely helpless. Stephen looked at him uncertainly. As the girl had said on the ride over, sometimes they carried these tricks too far. He felt sorry for Tiny Bledsoe because whatever the Coolihans had in mind it would not be pleasant. He supposed this was none of his business but he decided to interfere anyhow. Reaching up, he grabbed the edge of the wagon box and clambered over. He got out his pocketknife and began sawing on Tiny Bledsoe's bonds.

"Thanks, Chief," Tiny Bledsoe said when he got the

gag out of his mouth. "Where did those two idiots go?"

"They went back to ambush your brother," Stephen replied.

As he spoke they heard the distant sound of a struggle and a half-shout of outrage.

"I guess they got him," Tiny Bledsoe said. "Just wait until they bring him over here and I'll bash their heads in."

They clambered out of the wagon and Tiny Bledsoe moved over to stand beside a huge maple tree.

"You stay out of this," he warned Stephen. "Get back well out of sight."

A minute later two figures appeared in the center of the farmyard, one of them carrying a struggling body over his shoulder. They paused while still some distance from the wagon, and one of them said to the other, "You go on in and tell Don that we're leaving, will you? And bring me a piece of pie or cake if you can. I'm hungry."

Tiny Bledsoe waited until the Coolihan boy had passed him and then he attacked from the rear. There was a mad scramble and a gurgle and all three figures rolled in the dust. Surprise proved a big help, and furthermore, Tiny Bledsoe was in no mood to treat his opponent gently. He put one hand over the Coolihan boy's mouth and with the other arm managed some sort of a headlock. When the dust cleared, Stephen saw that Tiny was sitting on top of the Coolihan boy, who was face down in the dirt.

"Make any noise and I'll break your arm," Tiny warned. Stephen limped forward and began sawing at the bonds of the other Bledsoe boy. In less than a minute he was free.

"What'll we do with him?" Tiny Bledsoe asked his brother. "Throw him in the horse trough?"

"I want to take a poke at him first," Big Boy Bledsoe said angrily.

"Why don't you tie him up the way they did you?" Steve suggested.

"Hey, that's a wonderful idea," Tiny said enthusiastically. "If we work fast and we're lucky, maybe we'll get them both."

Using the pieces of rope that had been around their own hands and feet, they quickly tied the Coolihan twin and stuffed his mouth with rags. Then they tossed him in the wagon and stood in the shadow of a tree and waited.

They did not have long to wait, for a moment later the other Coolihan twin appeared eating a piece of pie that was in his right hand and carefully carrying another piece for his brother in his left. As he passed the tree, both of the Bledsoes jumped on his back. In a moment they had him on the ground while Stephen looked sorrowfully at the two pieces of pie that had fallen in the dust. They found some additional rope and bound the second Coolihan twin as securely as the first, and tossed him in beside his brother.

"This is too good to be true," Big Boy Bledsoe said happily. "What are we going to do with them?"

"I wonder what they were going to do with us?" Tiny Bledsoe said thoughtfully.

As they discussed various fiendish ideas, they walked

slowly toward the house. Stephen limped along beside them. As they neared the door of the kitchen, Stephen hung behind. He wanted to know what happened, but he had no intention of entering the room while Hannah Frisbee was there.

"If we go in, Don will know that something's happened and he'll go out and cut them loose," Tiny Bledsoe pointed out.

"I know!" his brother said, slapping his thigh with glee. "We'll send Steve in to give him a message from the Coolihans. They've changed their plans and are going to pull some other trick so Don is supposed to drive on down to the road and they'll meet him later."

"Wonderful idea!" said Tiny happily. "He'll drive off thinking he has us."

He turned to Stephen. "Have you got that, Steve? You go in and say the Coolihans asked you to give Don a message."

Stephen was busily searching for a reasonable excuse for not going inside when he heard his name mentioned in the kitchen.

"Where's Steve?" Dan Monroe asked. "He's disappeared. I wonder if he had anything to eat?"

"Steve who?" Mrs. Gault asked.

"I don't know his last name," Dan confessed. "He's been working with Bob Simms, who runs the threshing rig on our circuit. Nice kid."

Stephen glanced through the kitchen window. Hannah

Frisbee was standing with a knife poised above a large chocolate cake looking intently at Dan Monroe. She had not missed a word.

"Is he lame?" he heard her cold voice ask.

Stephen squared his shoulders and turned toward the two Bledsoe boys.

"I've got it straight," he assured them. "I'll give him the message."

He opened the door and limped inside. He paused just inside the doorway and looked calmly around the room. He accepted his lameness with resignation most of the time but now he bitterly resented that clumsy right foot. He wanted to be able to march forward straight and proud and look Hannah in the eye. However, one had to do the best he could with what he had. He took a deep breath and started across the room to deliver his message.

Chapter XII

Clearing Skies

I T WAS after one o'clock when Stephen reached the
Goodwin home that night. He did not want to
awaken the Goodwins, so instead of going to the bedroom which they had given him, he climbed up the
ladder into the haymow and stretched out on the soft,
sweet-smelling hay. The big mow door at the end of the
huge barn was open and he could lie on his back and look
out at the stars. Although it was late, he did not feel sleepy.
For several hours he thought about what he should do but
came to no conclusions. About four o'clock he finally
drifted off to sleep.

He did not awaken until almost nine the next morning.
In spite of the late hour Mrs. Goodwin insisted on cooking
him a breakfast of scrambled eggs, ham, fried potatoes,
biscuits, and gravy. After he had finished his breakfast
Stephen went out to talk with Simms, who was working on
his beloved engine.

"What do you think she'll do?" he asked Simms, after
he had told his story.

"I don't know," Simms admitted, "but whatever she does it will cause trouble, I'll guarantee that."

Shortly before noon they had their answer. Hannah Frisbee appeared in a buggy and with her was a deputy sheriff. They drove up beside the engine where Simms and Stephen were working and the sheriff climbed down. Hannah sat in the buggy watching with an air of prim righteousness.

"Are you Stephen McGowan?" the sheriff asked.

"Yes."

"And are you the ward of Mrs. Frisbee and her husband?"

"I don't know whether I'm their ward or not," Stephen replied. "I was living with them up until about a month ago."

"What'd you run away for?" the sheriff asked.

"Because I didn't like it there," Stephen answered simply. "I thought I'd get a job."

"That drifter there probably lured him away," Hannah said, with a glance of contempt at Simms.

Simms was still working on his engine. He paused, looked at Hannah, and said mildly, "Mrs. Frisbee, any man with a big steam engine and a threshing rig couldn't drift very far or very fast and I didn't lure Stephen away."

"I didn't even know where he was," Stephen said. "I caught a ride in this general direction, asked around, and finally found him. What's more, I want to stay with him."

"Well, you haven't got much choice in the matter," the

sheriff observed. "You're a minor. In fact, you're not even sixteen, so you'd better go get your things and go along with Mrs. Frisbee."

Stephen looked at Simms, but Simms said nothing. Stephen turned and walked slowly toward the house. It took only a minute for him to stuff his few belongings in a bag. He was about to leave the room when Simms came up the stairs. The lanky man with the birthmark stood hesitantly in the doorway nervously turning his big straw hat in his hands.

"I guess we're helpless," he said finally. "I can't see any way I can stop them from making you go along. It's a shame, though, 'cause I know how much you hate to go back."

Stephen looked out of the window and tried to hide the tears that were forming in his eyes.

"I'm afraid of her," he said at last. "I suppose I sound like a coward, but I'm afraid of her."

"I know what you mean," Simms said.

"It wouldn't be so bad if my mother hadn't been so different from her," Stephen said, feeling suddenly very sorry for himself.

"Yes, it would. It would be worse," Simms said unexpectedly. "There's nothing can take the place of a mother you love but the next best thing is the memory of one. Be thankful you have that. I know what I'm talking about because I haven't. I never liked my mother. She wasn't as bad as Hannah but I don't have much I want to remember about her or my childhood."

"I'm sorry," Stephen said, forgetting his own troubles for an instant.

"We have a lot of things in common," Simms said with a twisted grin. "We made a good team. I was hoping we could stay together."

"So was I," Stephen said. He picked up his bag of clothes and held out his hand. "Thanks for giving me a job."

"I ought to thank you," Simms said. "I don't know how I would have run the rig without you." He produced a fat wallet and pulled out forty dollars.

"I don't want any money," Stephen protested.

"I would have paid a man a good deal more than that," Simms said, "and you did the work of a man. Here, take it, but put it someplace and keep it out of sight of Hannah."

Stephen didn't argue. He took the money and placed it carefully in his watch pocket. "Send me a card now and then, will you, so I'll know where you are?"

Simms nodded. "I'll do that, and what's more I'll be back to Black Hawk sometime this fall. You can depend on that. Tell your Uncle Alf that I'll be by to talk to him. And don't let this get you down; sooner or later we'll figure a way out."

Stephen and Hannah left that afternoon on the eastbound train for Black Hawk. Hannah had very little to say during the long trip but her cold, hostile silence bothered Stephen more than anything she could have said. He had the uneasy feeling that she was forcing him to return to Black Hawk because she wanted revenge. He could see no other reason when she both disliked him and objected to the extra work he caused.

It was the middle of the night when they arrived in Black Hawk. Alf Frisbee met them at the station. He said little but gave Stephen's hand a friendly squeeze. It was not until the following morning at the livery stable that they were able to talk privately.

"I'm glad you're back, Stephen," Alf said awkwardly. "Maybe I haven't shown it much, and I suppose I haven't told you, but you mean a lot to me. I'm sorry you aren't happy here and I wish I could promise you that things will be different, but I can't."

"I've enjoyed being here at the stable and working with you," Stephen said. "I just thought that everybody'd be happier if I wasn't in the way."

"You weren't in the way," Alf protested. "I've missed you, but I want you to know that I wouldn't have made you come back."

"Why did Hannah do it?" Stephen asked.

"Hannah's not exactly an affectionate woman," Alf said. "I suppose in a way it's been a good thing that we never had any children because she just isn't cut out for a mother. But Hannah does her duty as she sees it and she figured it just wasn't right for a boy your age to be wandering around the country with a threshing rig. You ought to finish your schooling, Stephen, and you can't do that unless you stay in one place."

Herb Bainbridge did not agree, however, that it was Hannah's devotion to duty that caused her to bring Stephen back to Black Hawk.

"I suppose a man has got to defend his wife," he said one day to Stephen, "and Alf must have seen something in Hannah when he married her, although for the life of me I can't figure out what it was. I think Hannah wanted you back here so she could try and run your life. She's one of those people who figure the good Lord put them on earth so they can tell other people what to do."

Stephen was certain that Hannah had no intention of forgetting the incident with the gypsy. He waited apprehensively for her to try to even the score. But the days passed and nothing happened. He grew more and more nervous as time went by, until finally he began to hope for the blow to fall. However, Hannah did nothing but maintain her attitude of cold hostility. She rarely spoke to Stephen except to criticize him, and she never missed a chance to belittle him in the presence of her husband. Finally Stephen realized that she did not plan revenge in one swift stroke. Instead, she planned to make him as miserable as possible day after day, indefinitely. She would avoid an open battle but would keep picking, picking, picking.

His defense was to spend every moment possible away from the house. He ate there and he slept there, and that was all. Most of his waking hours were spent at the livery stable. When there was time he went on long rides around the countryside on Copper Lady.

As the days passed with no violent words or open argu-
ments between Hannah and Stephen, Alf Frisbee con-
cluded that they had arrived at some sort of truce. Stephen
knew better. It was merely a stalemate in the silent struggle
between them and the storm clouds were always just over
the horizon. One Saturday morning he arose feeling
particularly apprehensive. Hannah was unusually irritable
at breakfast and he watched her warily.

As he worked through the morning at the livery stable
the uneasy feeling persisted. Shortly after lunch he saddled
Copper Lady and rode out south of town to pick up a
buggy and team that had been rented earlier in the day.
As he reached the open country he realized suddenly that
his uneasiness was due in part at least to the weather. The
atmosphere was close and heavy and there was an odd
yellowish cast to the light. The sun, which was normally
hot and brilliant, was hazy and murky. For some reason it
seemed oddly difficult to breathe, as though he were
penned in a close, stuffy room.

When he reached his destination he tied Copper Lady
behind the buggy and immediately started back to town.
As he drove along Main Street he realized that he was not
the only one disturbed by the weather. Men stood in the
streets looking up at the sky nervously, while others
gathered in small clusters to talk. Herb Bainbridge, Alf
Frisbee, and two other men stood in front of the livery
stable.

"Why's everyone out in the street?" Stephen asked as he drove in through the big doors.

"They don't like the looks of things," Alf replied.

"Why?" Stephen asked.

"When you get a yellowish sort of sky this way, and that close feeling in the air, it's no good," Alf said, shaking his head. He looked around the big gloomy stable thoughtfully. "Well, there's nothing much I can do except hope for the best."

"What do you expect will happen?" Stephen asked.

"Twister," Alf replied.

"What's a twister?"

"Cyclone."

There was an excited shout from the street. Alf tied the team to the nearest post and hurried outside. Stephen slipped the saddle off Copper Lady, put her in the stall, and then hurried toward the big doors himself. Half the townspeople were gathered in the center of the wide, dusty street looking excitedly toward the southwest.

At first Stephen was unable to see the cause of all the furor. Then someone pointed out a dark spot, barely visible over the tops of the trees. It was a dark cloud, but it was shaped like a funnel. It seemed oddly small to be the cause of so much excitement, but as Stephen watched, he, too, caught the virus of fear and excitement.

The cloud was approaching and moving to the left at the same time. Finally it was directly to the south and could be seen down the vista of the long, straight street. Stephen realized suddenly that the funnel was really a cone that was whirling round and round and round with terrifying speed. Stretching downward from its point was a long, thin black line which went all the way to the ground.

"It's going to go over toward the left of us," someone remarked.

They all watched in silent fascination, gazing intently at the whirling cone as though hypnotized. Finally Herb Bainbridge's voice broke the trance.

"That's not going to the left of us at all," he said grimly. "It's coming right through town and it's time we headed for cover."

The group of people seemed to evaporate. One minute there was a large crowd and then suddenly everyone was gone. Alf Frisbee grasped Stephen by the arm and hurried him through the doors into the livery stable.

"Right on out the back," he said.

Moving as fast as his foot would permit him, Stephen went out the back door and across the alley toward the house.

"I'll get Hannah," Alf said. "You go on and get inside."

Stephen knew that Alf did not mean inside the house but inside the storm cellar. The storm cellar was a small underground cave which was normally used as a root cellar. Nothing showed above the ground but a small hump of earth. Stephen descended the stone steps, pushed open the heavy wooden door, ducked down, and went inside. A minute later Hannah Frisbee came down the steps and behind her Stephen could see Alf Frisbee's legs. She entered the dim interior of the cellar but Alf remained standing just outside.

"Come on in and close the door," Hannah snapped.

Alf started to obey orders, but halfway through the door he paused.

"It looks like it's coming straight through the middle of town," he said. "I think I'll go over to the stable and turn the horses loose."

"Are you crazy?" Hannah asked. "They'll be as safe there as anywhere else outside of a storm cellar."

"No, they won't," Alf said. "There's quite a bit of hay up there in the mow. If this twister gives the building much of a wrench, that hay could drop down on top of them. If the beams didn't break their backs, the hay would smother them."

He turned and started up the steps. Hannah hurried to the door after him.

"Come back, you fool!" she screamed. "You haven't time!"

There was no reply from Alf, but Stephen could hear the sudden ominous sound of a fast-rising wind. Hannah looked up at the sky and stark fear showed in her face. She grabbed the big door with both hands and slammed it hard. The inside of the cellar was in sudden and complete darkness.

"Maybe I ought to go help him," Stephen suggested.

"Don't you dare open that door!" Hannah said in an

almost hysterical scream. "We'll both be killed!"

Even through the thick plank door they could hear the wind screaming overhead. There was nothing to do but hope and pray and wait. With the slowness of eternity the minutes passed. Finally the roaring wind began to subside and the heavy, oppressive pressure of the air began to ease.

"It seems to have pretty well quieted down now," Stephen observed. He moved past Hannah, until his hand was on the door. "Is it all right to open it?" he asked.

"I guess so," Hannah replied in a strangely subdued voice. "Whatever was going to happen has happened, I suppose."

Stephen opened the door and gazed outside. To his surprise a pelting rain was falling. The wind had subsided to a stiff breeze. Disregarding the rain, he ascended a few steps and looked around him.

At first glance it appeared that the twister had done little damage. Black Hawk seemed much the same, but then he began to observe odd discrepancies. The tall steeple of the Methodist church had vanished completely. One of the elevators had lost its cupola. Branches had been wrenched from trees and pieces of wreckage and debris were scattered up and down the alley. Stephen looked closely at the rear of the stable and decided that it had survived the storm safely. Then he realized with sudden dread that something had happened to the front of the building. The big square false front had been wrenched completely out of shape. Without waiting to inform Hannah, he hurried up the stairs and toward the rear of the stable.

The back door of the big building was open and huddled just inside were ten or twelve terrified horses. He managed to get by them and went on toward the office. Halfway there he stopped. Alf's fears had been realized. Some of the beams supporting the haymow had dropped, and the huge weight of hay had fallen to the ground floor.

"Uncle Alf," he called. "Uncle Alf, where are you?"

Four hours later they found Alf Frisbee. He had been pinned beneath a falling beam. The beam had provided a small pocket of air around his head and had kept him from being smothered. His chest had been crushed and he was badly injured. Even as they removed him from the debris, everyone knew that he could not live long. They used the door of the office which had been ripped from its hinges as a stretcher and they carried him across the alley to his home. He was placed on the couch in the parlor where Dr. Kirk gave him something to relieve his pain.

Stephen sat unhappily in the kitchen, hoping and praying that Alf would live but knowing in his heart that there was little hope. About two-thirty Alf asked to see him. Apparently the dying man had asked Hannah to leave, because she left the room as Stephen entered. Alf motioned for him to take the chair beside the couch.

"There are some things I want to tell you," he said. "Some things I want to explain."

"Should he talk?" Stephen asked Dr. Kirk, who was closing his black bag and was about to leave.

"It'll make very little difference," Dr. Kirk said. "He'll feel better if he's able to say what he has to say."

"I haven't been much of a man, Steve," Alf Frisbee said. "I guess I've been pretty much of a coward most of my life."

"You haven't either," Stephen protested.

Alf waved him to silence. "Yes, I have. I've allowed Hannah to rule me all our married life and make me do things that I didn't want and I knew weren't right." He held up a hand to stop Stephen's protests. "Listen and let me finish.

"Your mother and I were very close. I knew she was going to run away with your father and I helped her do it. Your grandparents were pretty strict and I knew they'd never let your mother marry your father. Later Ma and Pa helped me start in the livery business, and several years after that they left the farm and everything they had to me. Half of everything really belonged to your mother and I should have given it to her then. Instead, I got the betting fever and lost the farm to Gus Van Derhoff. I've always felt that I treated my sister mighty poor. Your mother had a pretty tough time of it in Chicago and I should have helped her. But if I'd sent her the money that I should have, Hannah would have known, and that's where I was a coward. I let Hannah keep me from doing what I should have done."

"I understand," Stephen said.

"Anyhow, one of the reasons I wanted that farm back

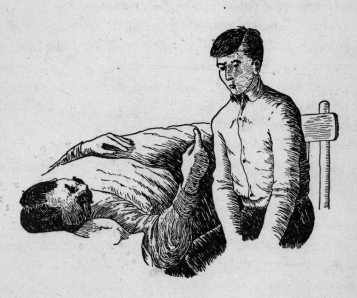

so badly was because I felt that someday it should belong to you."

He paused, closed his eyes, and Stephen looked in alarm at Dr. Kirk. The doctor started toward the couch and then stopped as Alf Frisbee opened his eyes again.

"When I went over to the county seat to record that deed, I took care of another detail. I made my will. I guess I knew that the only time I'd ever find courage to give you what I really felt was yours would be when I died. Nothing Hannah could say or do could stop me then. Tompkins down at the bank has my will. In it I left the entire farm to you. Hannah gets the livery stable and the house here, and you get the farm."

Again Alf Frisbee closed his eyes. Stephen wanted to protest, to insist that Alf was going to get well, that he shouldn't talk about dying or about his will, but he knew that such protests would be meaningless.

"And Copper Lady," Alf Frisbee said without opening his eyes. "I said in my will that if I still had her she was to belong to you."

"Copper Lady?" Stephen said in surprise.

Alf smiled slightly. "Yes, I bought her shortly after Simms came here. I kept it a secret partly because I didn't want Gus Van Derhoff to know I owned a race horse. He'd have watched her too closely. Mainly, though, I guess it was just a case of being scared of Hannah again." He smiled again and said, "It's funny, but it seems like I've spent a lot of my life hiding things because I've been afraid of Hannah. It's not much of a way for a man to live, Stephen."

"I'll take good care of Copper Lady," Stephen promised.

"I know you will," Alf said. He held out a hand, and Stephen grasped it. "You're a good boy and I'm proud to have you as my nephew. Let Gus Van Derhoff operate the farm for you on shares. He's a good farmer and he's an honest man." He looked at Dr. Kirk and said, "How much longer do you think I have, Doctor?"

"I don't know," Dr. Kirk answered honestly. "A few hours, perhaps."

Alf smiled. "Well, in spite of some regrets, I've enjoyed

myself and you gave me one of the greatest moments in my life, Steve, when you won that race."

Alf Frisbee died late in the afternoon and through the mysterious means by which news travels in small towns, his passing was soon known to everyone. Herb Bainbridge appeared and invited Stephen to spend the next few days at his home. Stephen accepted gratefully and packed his suitcase. Although he told Hannah that he was merely leaving for a day or two, they both knew that he was moving out permanently.

Mr. Tompkins asked him to come down to the bank the day after the funeral. Hannah was there when he arrived, and in the privacy of Mr. Tompkins's office the will was opened and read. Alf Frisbee had told Hannah nothing about the provisions of this new will and she was amazed and furious when she learned that Stephen had inherited the farm. She threatened to contest the will, but as Mr. Tompkins told Stephen later, there was nothing she could do.

"I'm appointed your legal guardian," he told Stephen. "But your uncle said nothing about who is to have actual custody of you. I suppose he assumed you'd keep on living with Hannah."

"I don't want to," Stephen said bluntly. "That's the last place in the world I want to live."

"Well, as you know, I'm a widower and I live at the hotel so I can't provide much in the way of a home for you myself. Let's both think it over for a few days before we come to a decision."

Stephen still had no ideas about where or with whom he would like to live, when Herb Bainbridge came home at noontime a few days later with the news that a steam engine had been seen four miles east of town.

"That must be your friend," he told Stephen. "He's touring around the countryside in that steam engine as though it were a surrey."

Stephen had shifted Copper Lady to a pasture near Herb Bainbridge's. He immediately saddled the little mare and rode off to investigate. Herb's surmise was correct, and he met Simms creeping slowly but surely along the road with his huge steam engine. It was hissing and clanking and puffing and the stack was spewing forth mighty clouds of black smoke. Simms was seated at the throttle viewing the countryside with calm contentment. When he saw Stephen, he waved happily.

"Told you I'd be back to see you before fall. Didn't think at the time, though, that I'd be driving Helen."

"Where are you going?" Stephen asked.

"To Black Hawk to see your Uncle Alf," Simms replied, "and then on north to a sawmill job."

He stopped his big engine and climbed down so that they could talk without shouting. Stephen told him the news about Alf Frisbee.

"I'm sorry to hear about Alf," Simms said. "The people you like die young and the mean ones live on forever.

Hannah will still be alive at ninety-two."

Simms called on Mr. Tompkins at the bank when it opened the next morning. He was closeted with him for almost two hours, and when he finally emerged he was smiling triumphantly. Stephen was waiting on the bench with Herb Bainbridge in front of the livery stable. Although the front end of the stable had been practically demolished, the bench was intact, and it was still occupied by its usual quota of loafers.

"Well, I convinced him," Simms said. "Saddle up your horse and we're ready to roll. Mr. Tompkins says that if that's what you want, you can come with me."

An hour later they were creeping along the road at a snail's pace headed northward. Black Hawk lay behind them, a clump of trees pierced by a few church spires. Copper Lady, who apparently considered steam engines as pleasant companions, had been tethered with a long lead to the rear of the engine and Stephen had climbed up beneath the canopy to talk with Simms for a while.

"How far is this sawmill job?" he asked.

"Oh, about a hundred and thirty or forty miles," Simms replied.

"A hundred and forty miles!" Stephen said incredulously. "Why, it'll take days to get there!"

Simms nodded. "What's your hurry? You're young."

"How'd you happen to pick a job so far away?"

"I wanted it," Simms replied. "We're going to be up near Rochester, Minnesota."

"Why do you want to go there?"

Simms was silent for a moment and then he said, "Do you remember when we had that talk and I said we were both sort of cripples and ought to stick together?" When Stephen nodded, he continued, "Well, I think we ought to stick together, but not because we're cripples. When you've got a cross to bear like this face or that foot of yours you have to make the best of it, but if you don't have to bear it, it seems sort of silly to keep on doing it. Some-time ago I asked Dr. Kirk to take a look at that foot of yours."

"He did look at it," Stephen said. "But I didn't know you'd asked him."

Simms nodded. "Well, I talked to him about it. He says that maybe something can be done. I don't want you to get your hopes too high, but there's a possibility. You'd have to wear some mighty uncomfortable braces for a long time, but I'd guess you'd be willing to do that if it would fix that foot."

"I certainly would," Stephen replied.

"Well, up there at Rochester they have a place called the Mayo Clinic with some of the best medical men in the world, so when I got a chance to get this sawmill job just outside of Rochester, I took it. I figured I'd try to persuade your Uncle Alf to let you go with me for the winter. As it worked out I had to persuade Mr. Tompkins instead. I don't know what we'll do about your schooling, but we'll work something out."

Stephen was too overwhelmed to think of anything to say for several minutes. He stared out across the green cornfields until he had control of his emotions.

"Why are you doing all this for me?" he asked.

"Well, you're always hearing how kids growing up need love and affection and someone who really takes an interest in them. I guess maybe that's right. What you don't hear, though, is that almost everyone, no matter what age they are, needs someone to love, someone to be interested in. This isn't a one-sided affair, Stephen. There hasn't been anyone who's cared a hoot and a holler about me for years. That hasn't bothered me. There hasn't been anyone that I cared about and that has bothered me, so you see I'm getting as much out of this as you are. Don't waste a lot of time trying to say that you're grateful. Instead, you just get on that horse of yours and get on up ahead to that bridge. Take a good look at it and see whether you think it will hold Helen here. If not, we'll have to turn at the next crossroad and make a detour."

Stephen got on his horse and went racing down the country road. Copper Lady was feeling frisky and wanted to run. The wind felt cool and kind as it swept past his cheeks. It was a wonderful sunlit world. He patted Copper Lady's neck fondly and said, "You're mine now, Lady." He smiled as he thought of Hannah Frisbee's remark. "If wishes were horses"—well, sometimes wishes were horses and e'en beggars might ride, or better still might someday walk like other men.

About the author . . .

KEITH ROBERTSON was born in Dows, Iowa, and has lived in Iowa, Minnesota, Wisconsin, Kansas, Oklahoma, Missouri, Pennsylvania and New Jersey.

He received his B.S. from the United States Naval Academy at Annapolis, Maryland. He spent a total of eleven years in the United States Navy, five on a destroyer in the Atlantic and Pacific oceans before and during World War II. At the end of the war he held the rank of commander. He is now a captain in the Naval Reserve.

Mr. Robertson is the author of many books for young people and has written technical booklets and manuals as well. While his principal activity is writing, Mr. Robertson and his family live on and operate a farm in Hopewell, New Jersey. He is president of the Hopewell Museum, which he feels is an unusually fine museum of early American village life.

Mrs. Robertson operates a rare-book business, specializing in garden and cook books. This has led Mr. Robertson to develop an interest in old books. The accumulation of books forced the Robertsons to move out of their old house and to settle in New Jersey at Booknoll Farm with their three children, Christina, twelve, Jeffry, nine, and Hope, six.

About IF WISHES WERE HORSES, Mr. Robertson says, ". . . the life and countryside described is much the same as that I knew in Iowa as a boy. Horses still did the work of the farming world and tractors were a rarity."